They both looked u

a seagull swooped down a little too close to their heads. She gasped and Micah clutched her body to his. He waved one hand in the air to frighten the bird away.

When it was gone, he didn't let go, and she didn't want him to. She was finally where she wanted to be ever since he'd set foot in her grandmother's restaurant.

She laid her cheek on his chest and inhaled. If he wore cologne, it was very lightly applied, which was fine with her. She preferred the scent of clean skin as opposed to scents splashed from a bottle.

"That was scary," she whispered, looping her arms around his waist. "But this feels nice."

Enclosed in his strong arms and with her head nestled against his muscular chest, she did not feel confined. She felt empowered, free to say what she felt in her heart.

Micah placed his palms on her cheeks and stared into her eyes. He closed his eyes and brought his lips to hers.

"I bet this will feel even better."

His kiss was sweet and tender, and she felt her body melt against his.

Dear Reader,

Since moving to New York City a few years ago, I've been able to enjoy eating at many of the area's wonderful restaurants. Sharing a meal is one of the best ways to get to know someone.

Micah Langston and Jasmine Kennedy share a love of food and family, and a fear of commitment. I hope you enjoy their journey as much as I enjoyed writing it.

Thank you for purchasing and reading *Winning Her Heart*. Follow me on Facebook or Twitter, or just check out my website for news about future releases.

Best,

Harmony

Winning HER Heart

Harmony Evans

HARLEQUIN® KIMANI™ ROMANCE

Recycling programs for this product may not exist in your area.

ISBN-13: 978-1-335-21669-4

Winning Her Heart

For questions and comments about the quality of this book please contact us at CustomerService@Harlequin.com.

HARLEQUIN®
www.Harlequin.com

Printed in U.S.A.

Harmony Evans received the 2013 Romance Slam Jam Emma Award for Debut Author of the Year. Her first book, *Lesson in Romance*, garnered two RT Reviewers' Choice Best Book Award nominations in 2012. She currently resides in New York City. Visit her at www.harmonyevans.com.

Books by Harmony Evans

Harlequin Kimani Romance

Lesson in Romance
Stealing Kisses
Loving Laney
When Morning Comes
Winning Her Love
Winning the Doctor
Winning Her Heart

Chapter 1

Almost there. Almost home.

Micah Langston shifted his sleek black convertible into fifth gear as it zipped along the Pacific Coast Highway north from San Francisco toward Bay Point.

The midafternoon sun beamed down on his head. The air was fresh and clean, and the convertible, though it was a rental, made him want one for his own.

He loved the feel of the wind sliding over his hair like invisible silk. The unadulterated freedom, riding rooftop down, exhilarated him.

Watch it, Micah, he warned himself, frowning slightly.

You could get used to this.

To his left, the Pacific Ocean beckoned. Magellan, the Portuguese explorer, had coined it *Mar Pacifico*, which means peaceful ocean. Micah glanced over at the endless expanse of blue, wondering if he'd ever feel a sense of peace. But he'd given his word. He had to give Bay Point one more chance.

Micah left his hometown over ten years ago to attend the famed Culinary Institute of America in Hyde Park, New York. Once he'd graduated, he rarely returned home, except for important family functions.

Instead, he'd spent his time focusing on his career.

By the time he was twenty-eight, he owned three successful restaurants in New York City, San Francisco and Portland, Oregon. As executive chef of each one, he created his own recipes, specializing in southern cuisine with a Latin twist. All the restaurants were branded Society Red, were immensely popular and garnered rave reviews. And for good reason; he was a damn good cook.

His older brother, Gregory Langston, the mayor of Bay Point, wanted him to open up a restaurant downtown. He had lured him back home with the promise of big tax breaks and potentially big profits. Mayor Langston was convinced that Micah's name would draw tourists year-round.

Micah exited the highway and headed east. In his mind, this trip was exploratory only. His brother might have a vision for the small beach town, but that didn't mean he agreed with it, or necessarily wanted to play a role.

Now, at only thirty years old, he wasn't sure Bay Point was the place to drop a permanent pin on all he had yet to accomplish in the culinary world.

But he loved his brother, so to appease him, he and his partners, who were also successful chefs, had gone ahead and purchased property in downtown Bay Point, at a very affordable price.

However, Micah had not decided if he wanted to actually install one of *his* restaurants there. His partners, who each had an equal stake, argued that since he was the most famous chef of the trio, his name and his restaurant would be the best option.

In other words, Micah was their golden ticket.

Work had already begun to restore the decrepit, seventy-five-year-old building. The exterior renovations would take several months, and they were having difficulty getting some of the permits approved. Micah was glad for the much-needed time to make a final decision.

A restaurant *would* be built in Bay Point, just not necessarily his. He wasn't making any promises to his brother, or anyone else for that matter. He loved his family, but his ambition had always come first, a trait that had made him very, very rich.

Micah turned onto Magnolia Avenue and his eyes widened. Since he'd last visited a couple of years ago, Bay Point had undergone significant development. There were fancy boutiques, luxury condominiums and a slew of new restaurants lining the main road into town.

"That's why I'm here," he muttered. "To check out the competition."

His first stop was 333 Magnolia Avenue, home of Lucy's Bar and Grille, a local favorite that had been around for as long as he could remember.

The restaurant was located directly across the street from his property, which he thought was a major bonus. What better way to advertise a new restaurant than to open up right across the street from an old, outdated one?

He angled the convertible into a parking spot right up front and smiled, finding it comical that Lucy's was even considered "competition." Though he did have fond memories of eating there when he was a teenager, it was more of a diner than a fine restaurant.

Micah walked inside and stopped in his tracks, shocked to find the dining room full. Though it was way past the lunch hour, the only seats available were at the bar.

A few heads turned as he made his way back. Being recognized always gave him a rush. He openly welcomed fame, but even more, the money and notoriety that came with it.

He slid onto a wooden bar stool that had seen better days, and reminded himself that the only appeal of the place was the food. His stomach rumbled as he inhaled the comforting scents of garlic, hot pepper sauce and olive oil. He'd grabbed a quick bite at the airport, but hadn't eaten since.

Several feet away, down a small hallway to his right, a door he knew led to the kitchen suddenly swung open. A woman emerged, holding a tray in one hand, high above her head.

She walked toward him, hips swaying side to side in the most tantalizing way. He envied the red-checkered apron riding shotgun on her short denim miniskirt. His lower body tensed and tightened, so much so that he was glad he was sitting down. Suddenly, Lucy's had more than one thing going for it.

The woman reached the bar and frowned. Micah noticed that there was no place to set the tray.

He half swiveled in his seat. "Allow me."

Facing her, without waiting for a response, he lifted the tray from her hands.

She cocked her head at him, gave a little smile and then served the elderly couple sitting on his left their meals.

When she was finished, he gave her back the tray, which she promptly stuck under her arm.

Since he was sitting right next to the pass-through to the bar, he lifted it, telling himself it was the courteous thing to do. But the truth was he just wanted to see her smile again.

With a nod, but not a smile, she skirted through, and he slowly released the counter into place.

She set the tray on top. "Thanks for your help. I'll take your order in a moment."

The southern accent he detected in her voice nestled into his senses as he watched her refill drinks and make sure customers were happy with their food.

Then, she took a rag and wiped down the counter in front of him.

"Sorry for the wait. Welcome to Lucy's."

Her T-shirt was black, V-necked, and her cleavage was as deep as her smile. The words *Ask Me if I Care* were emblazoned across the front in thin silvery cursive.

As she handed him a menu, her breasts riffed against the glossy surface of the bar.

Though it was difficult, he managed to avert his eyes as she poured him a glass of water, but his hard-on tightened uncomfortably as though she were standing in front of him, naked.

A customer a few bar stools down asked her a question and she turned her face away. He gave in to temptation, stealing the moment to soak up the woman's tantalizing figure.

She was petite and curvy. Short hair spiked in a hip style. Bangs asymmetrical, the longer side skimmed her left eyebrow. Daring him to brush them away so he could see the color of her eyes.

She set a glass of water down in front of him. "Can I tell you about today's specials?"

As she rattled them off, a pang of desire hit him, confused him.

That voice. That body.

She was the exact opposite of the model-thin types that normally interested him, at least for a night.

"Perhaps," he said, wanting her to linger. "What's looking good today?"

Besides you, he thought, biting back the words.

He wanted to tease her, to let her know that he found her very attractive, but it felt disrespectful to do that in a place like Lucy's.

"All the food is good here," she continued. "But we've been real busy today and have already run out of some of the menu items. Tell me what you want, and I'll check in with the kitchen to see if we still have it."

Micah set his menu aside. He already knew what he wanted, besides the luscious woman in front of him.

"How about one of Lucy's famous jerk chicken sandwiches?"

She arched a perfectly curved brow. "Oh, so you've heard about those?"

"I've had one or two in my lifetime. I grew up in Bay Point, and used to eat here frequently when I was a teenager."

"Hmm," she replied, her eyes roaming his face. "You don't look much older than that now."

"Thank you. I guess I age well."

He gave her his most disarming smile, happy that his boyish good looks had netted him another fine catch.

"I'm Micah Langston. And you are?"

"Jasmine Kennedy."

He reached out his hand, and her palm felt cool to the touch. "Pleasure to meet you."

"Langston." She tilted her head. "Are you any relation to—?"

"The mayor? He's my older brother."

Jasmine's cheeks dimpled and seemed to light up her face.

"The rumors are true then. Good looks do run in the family."

He leaned back a little. Her flirtatious compliment spiraled through him, warming his insides, catching him off guard, though he suspected she didn't mean a word of it.

Seconds later, he chided himself. When was the last time he ever cared what any woman thought about him?

"I like you already."

She smiled and laid down a napkin, followed by a knife, fork and spoon on top. "I'll bet you'll like me even more if we have any jerk chicken left. Let me go see. Be right back."

He turned his head and watched her leave. Her miniskirt hugged her curves so tight he wished he had X-ray eyes.

Her hip bumped against the kitchen door, causing it to swing open. When she disappeared behind it, it was like all the air had gone out of the room with her.

Micah gulped down some water, icy cold, but not cold enough to calm the lust she had unknowingly kindled.

To distract himself, he glanced around the restaurant.

The decor hadn't changed much from when he was a kid. Autographed photos of movies stars he didn't recognize. African masks draped with Mardi Gras beads. Old porcelain signs that were likely reproductions and other so-called antique treasures cluttered the walls.

He wrinkled his nose. So different from his taste. He favored sleek, modern designs allowing his customers to focus on what was most important—the food.

"I thought I heard a Langston out here."

He got off his chair and gave Lucy Dee Diller, the owner of the diner, a peck on the cheek. The aromatic scent of incense and coffee beans wafted over him. Her raspy voice had deepened, making her southern accent even more apparent. He wondered if she still smoked unfiltered cigarettes, and hoped she didn't.

Moments later, Jasmine was back, plate in hand. When he saw what was on it, he wanted to kiss her.

"Is that what I think it is?"

Lucy took the plate from Jasmine and slid it in front of him. "My famous jerk chicken sandwich with apple chutney and hand-sliced sweet potato fries."

Jasmine winked. "How do you like me now?"

"Like? I think I'm in love." He grinned at the two women, and then pointed at the food. "With all three of you."

Lucy laughed. "Didn't I tell you, Jasmine? Just like a Langston. You're all flirts, though your brother not so much because he's married."

Steam curled up from his fries. He could barely wait to dig in.

"After all these years, I'm surprised you still recognize me."

Lucy nodded. "Of course, I do! And not just because you've been on television."

"You're on television?" Jasmine asked.

Her voice held a note of disbelief that threatened to irk his ego. Micah shrugged, as if it was no big deal, even though to him, it was. He considered being on TV one of his greatest accomplishments.

She lifted the pass-through, and Lucy joined her behind the bar.

"Don't you know, honey? Micah is famous."

"Ever hear of *High Stakes Chef*?" he asked. "That's the name of the show."

Jasmine shook her head defiantly. "I don't watch television."

Lucy cut in, nudging the plate closer. "I remember your appetite and I don't like to see any man starve, famous or not. I made that sandwich just how you like it."

"With extra pepper sauce?"

At Lucy's nod, he picked up the sandwich and opened his mouth to take a bite.

"Uh-uh. Not yet. Napkin in the collar, please," Lucy scolded, unfolding one and doing the honors. "You know the drill. I'm not paying for your laundry."

When she was done, Micah grinned and fought to roll his eyes as he smoothed the napkin over his clean white button-down shirt. He wasn't a teenager anymore, but apparently Jasmine thought he looked like one, and Lucy thought he ate like one.

"Now, you eat," Lucy said.

He took a bite. "Mmm…this is as delicious and—" he paused to swallow and wipe some sauce from his lips "—as messy as I remember."

"I'm surprised you didn't order it that way," Lucy said.

"I've been a little distracted ever since I walked in," he replied, temporarily forgetting his hunger for food.

He looked up and caught Jasmine watching him, a little smile on her lips, as she poured a draft beer.

Lucy glanced between the two and narrowed her eyes. Known around town for having psychic abilities, Micah wondered if she saw the spark between him and Jasmine, or if it was just his imagination.

"Don't you go taking up my granddaughter's time," she warned. She tossed her head to the side and flattened one hand on the bar. "She has other customers and besides, she belongs to me."

Her voice, though kind, seemed overly protective. What did the woman think he was going to do? Kidnap the girl?

Micah lifted both hands up, hoping to quell Lucy's fears.

"Hold up. You have a granddaughter?"

He didn't even know Lucy had children. On the other hand, he wasn't surprised. He wasn't the type to delve into someone's personal life or even listen to the gossip that ran rampant in the small town.

"Isn't she beautiful?" She beamed a megawatt grin, followed by a dismayed frown. "Wait. Don't answer that. Just eat."

Between mouthfuls, he said, "You're both beautiful. Must run in *your* family."

Jasmine wiped her hands and leaned against the back of the bar. "I didn't want to believe you, but you're right, Gram. He's just like a Langston. A total flirt."

He put his sandwich down. "Takes one to know one," he teased good-naturedly, unable to help himself.

"Come on, you two. Break it up," Lucy said, waving her hands like a referee.

His eyes caught Jasmine's again, and he shrugged in spite of the flame of interest he saw there. It was time to change the subject before he got into trouble.

"How long have you owned the diner, Lucy?"

"Over fifty years. I moved to Bay Point when I was twenty-two years old."

"That's the same age I was when I opened up my first

restaurant," he exclaimed, surprised he had something in common with the feisty woman. "Now I have three."

Jasmine whistled. "Three restaurants!"

"It's not easy, but somehow I make it work."

"One is enough for me," Lucy said. "I'm so blessed that Jasmine moved here to help out."

"Oh? How long have you been in Bay Point?"

"Only a few months."

"She's been a godsend," Lucy said, looking over her shoulder as she rang up a customer. "I don't know what I would do without her."

"It's been about two years since I've been back in Bay Point," Micah said, trying a more direct track to get the information he needed. He'd almost forgotten why he'd stopped there in the first place.

Although the restaurant appeared to be doing well, he knew that keeping it that way was tough. If he did choose to open up his own across the street, Lucy's customers would have a choice. He was confident that most would choose to spend their hard earned dollars at Society Red.

"Things sure have changed. There are lots of new restaurants in town. Have they affected your business? Have you lost any customers?"

Jasmine cut in, her tone sharp. "That's none of your—"

Lucy turned and laid a hand on her granddaughter's arm. "Mind your manners."

"I mean. We're doing fine," Jasmine amended, folding her arms.

Micah wiped his mouth with his napkin, hiding his

frown of concern. Without meaning to, he'd stepped onto some invisible battleground between the two women.

He sighed inwardly. Though he was curious, Jasmine was right. It *was* none of his business.

"Lunch is our best time, though dinner is pretty steady, too," Lucy added as she lifted the pass-through. "I'd better get back and start prepping tonight's specials."

"Anything I can do to help?" he offered. "I know my way around a kitchen."

"Thanks, but no." Lucy gave him a quick hug. "Careful what you ask for Micah or we'll find something for you to do around here eventually. Won't we, Jasmine?"

Micah finished his sandwich while Jasmine took care of other customers at the bar.

When she returned, she cleared away his empty plate and placed it underneath the counter.

"How long are you in town?" she asked.

"I'm just visiting. I've got to get back to Portland in a few days."

"Is that where you live now?"

He shrugged. "Sometimes. I actually have an apartment in each city where I have a restaurant, so Portland, Chicago and New York City. I bounce around a lot."

"Sounds like fun, but I prefer to call one place home."

"You've only been here a little while. Is Bay Point 'home' for you already?" he teased.

"Time will tell." A shadow crossed her face, and he sensed she was unhappy. "My grandmother needs me."

She laid his bill on the counter. “I hope you enjoyed everything.”

He barely glanced at the amount and reached into his back pocket for his wallet, keeping his eyes on hers. “I did, and if I said something that offended you earlier, I’m sorry.”

Jasmine bit her lip and she seemed nervous. “You didn’t. I’m just protective of her, that’s all.”

“And she seems protective of you,” he said, handing over his platinum credit card. “Sounds like she really relies on you.”

“Lunchtime is busy and she needs the help.”

She shrugged her shoulders, then glanced over at the kitchen. “But I do more than pour drinks, she’s been doing the books by herself all these years, by hand no less. I’m bringing her into the 21st century.”

“Kicking and screaming?”

Jasmine laughed. “Oh, yeah. Definitely.”

“That’s wonderful. Do you help with the cooking too?”

“No way. I try to stay out of the kitchen as much as possible.”

She asked him if he wanted anything else, and he shook his head. He had other things to do that afternoon, but he also didn’t want their conversation to end.

“I could give you a cooking lesson.”

Jasmine pursed her lips. “Oh really? Can you give me an idea of what the first class would be like, so I can judge if I’m interested?”

“How about I teach you how to make homemade spaghetti sauce? And then how to cook the perfect pasta al dente? There's an art to cooking, you know."

Her half smile was sexy and dismissive at the same time. "Thanks, but with all I have to do around here, I don't think I have time."

She handed him the receipt, which he quickly signed. She tried to reach for his pen, but he held on to it.

"Wait. Before I go, I have something to ask you."

Jasmine furrowed her brow, but he couldn't tell if she was annoyed or curious.

"What is it?"

"Do you?"

He watched her face, deliberately being obtuse.

"Do I what?" she repeated, drawing out the words as if she didn't understand.

"Care." He pointed at her with the pen. "Your T-shirt says *Ask Me if I Care.* So, I'm asking. Do you care?"

She stared into his eyes, challenging him. "That's an odd question to ask someone you just met."

"Let's just say, I care about the answer."

Smiling, she lifted her chin. "Rub the crystal ball and see."

"That old thing is still here?"

He glanced toward the door surprised that he hadn't noticed the large glass orb nestled on a gold-columned pedestal near the front of the restaurant when he'd first walked in.

Locals touched it on their way in or out, hoping it would bring them good luck. He remembered giving the thing a good rub on the night of his senior prom, hoping he'd get lucky with his date. But she'd slapped him in the face when he made his move. He didn't even make it through the first kiss.

Over the years, his luck had changed. He had no trouble seducing any woman that he wanted, and Jasmine Kennedy would be no exception.

He gave her a large tip, and added his phone number before handing the receipt and the pen back to her.

"What's that sly grin for?" she asked.

"Call me and find out."

Micah winked and felt her eyes linger on his back as he headed toward the front of the restaurant. He knew she was waiting to see if he would touch the crystal ball.

But he refused, and sailed right past it. He wasn't a superstitious man, just a cautious one, and he didn't believe in magic. Just hard work.

The sun nearly blinded him when he emerged from the poorly lit restaurant. He'd forgotten his sunglasses in the car, so he shaded his eyes with his right hand and looked across the street at his building.

There was brown paper on the windows and the scaffolding was up, but no construction workers in sight. Checking his watch, he saw that it was nearly three o'clock. Were they already done for the day?

He stuck his hands in his pockets and jingled his keys, debating whether to check on the renovation, as he'd originally intended. He was expected for dinner at his family's beach estate at five o'clock, but wanted to get there early for a relaxing shower and shave.

Temporary lodging in his boyhood bedroom, he told himself.

At this point in his life, he just wasn't sure if his

hometown was even worthy of his time, talent and money.

He traveled regularly, living out of one suitcase, trying new cuisines and meeting new people around the world. He loved his lifestyle too much to be snagged down in one place, with one woman.

Micah looked back over his shoulder at Lucy's, and decided to visit his building later that evening, and check out the interior instead. There was a back entrance he could use to avoid attracting attention.

He got into his convertible and, after verifying that the road was clear, backed out.

All the way to his parents' house, he denied that it was because of Jasmine that he had changed his plans.

"My, my, Micah. Talk about afternoon delight!"

The man had left her a twenty-dollar tip on a ten-dollar meal. She couldn't decide whether he was a big spender or just trying to leave a big impression. He didn't need to wave around his money. All he needed to make heads turn was to walk into a room.

Jasmine hurried to the front of the restaurant. She bumped one of the empty rattan dining chairs to the side with her hip and positioned herself at the window. The gold curtain rings that held red-checkered café curtains pressed against her cleavage as she peeked outside.

A local construction worker sitting the next table over cackled at her. She ignored him, though she could feel his eyes ogling her miniskirted behind. He'd finished two orders of buffalo chicken wings and a pitcher of beer, and she knew from experience that she'd get nothing from him but trouble.

"Just one last look. That's all I need."

She clicked her tongue against the back of her teeth.

Micah Langston was just the break she needed in the middle of a busy day.

Handsome, sexy and not planning to stick around.

His clean-shaven, medium brown tone skin was unlined and appeared as smooth as a baby. His nose was a little smaller than she liked, but still fit with his oval-shaped face that angled at his jaws.

He appeared to be in his late twenties, maybe early thirties. She didn't see him pull out any reading glasses, and the piercing way he was looking at her made her think he could see just fine.

She wondered if the flecks of gray in his close-cut black hair were due to heredity, stress or age. She was twenty-three, so if they hooked up, they would be pretty close in age.

Those hazel eyes with specks of deep blue had sunk into hers, and she felt a little like when she slipped on her favorite fuzzy socks at night after a long day on her feet—warm, safe and a little thankful.

Micah had full lips that he knew to close when he munched on his food, unlike some of the customers that ate at Lucy's. Some of the things she'd seen since arriving at her grandmother's restaurant made her cringe even now. Just because it was cheap didn't mean it was okay to leave one's manners outside.

The black Audi proved he had terrific taste in cars, and the rental plates screamed just passing through.

Fine man, he was. Very fine.

She watched Micah slide his sunglasses over his nose, and check his rearview mirror, but not for his reflection.

A man that looked like him did not need to check his appearance, Jasmine thought. He was perfect.

She pressed the palm of her hand to the back of her neck. Her skin was hot, her secret gauge that indicated she was equally hot for a man, double verifying the exquisite pull in her loins that she felt when she first laid eyes on Micah.

He watched for cars, of which there were some crisscrossing the road, before pulling out onto Magnolia Avenue, heading west toward the beach.

She sighed and put one hand on her hip, watching until he disappeared.

"Get away from that window," her grandmother said, picking up a set of rooster-shaped salt and pepper shakers from an empty booth. "Never let a man know you're interested."

Jasmine turned and plastered an innocent smile on her face. "I'm not interested and besides, he's gone."

"Excuse me, ma'am."

She moved out of the way so Donnie, one of the busboys, could clear a table that was recently vacated. His arms stretched here and there removing every dish and piece of silverware into a square plastic tub.

As soon as he was done, Lucy slapped a wet rag down on the table and started to scrub.

"Great. A man like Micah Langston is no good for you."

Jasmine spotted another patron in the corner gesturing for a check, and hurried over. After she'd run their credit card and provided the receipt, she joined Lucy back behind the bar.

"What do you mean that Micah is no good for me? I thought the Langstons were a little like royalty in this town."

Lucy cocked a brow. "Just because Gregory is the mayor?"

Jasmine shrugged, placing a used beer glass on a tray under the bar.

Two years ago, Jasmine had graduated with honors from Tulane University with a degree in business administration, and a minor in accounting. Because of her strong internship history, she was lucky enough to land a job with a small advertising agency in the French Quarter as a junior account manager.

The pay was decent, the work interesting. She'd enjoyed helping the agency's clients, who were mostly restaurants, shops and historical sites, with their marketing strategy in hopes of attracting increased numbers of tourists to their respective businesses.

Then one night she'd stayed until almost midnight to help finalize a new business pitch. Her boss put his hand on her thigh, and she gave him a right hook across his leering mouth, and she never went back. Broke her lease and used her rent money to fly one-way to California.

"The Langstons have been here for generations," Lucy continued. "Micah is the only one who, after college, didn't come back to stay."

"He probably figured you were the best chef in town, so why stay here and get his butt beat?"

Lucy patted Jasmine's cheek, and she relished the touch of her grandmother's hand.

"You're kind to flatter me, but I'm not the one who is on television, am I?"

"Did you ever want fame and fortune?"

Lucy shook her head. "No, I moved to Bay Point to brush shoulders with both from time to time."

"The town used to be a weekend getaway for the stars, wasn't it?"

Lucy wiped down the bar and smiled wistfully. "I've seen my fair share of Hollywood royalty during the almost fifty years this restaurant has been open."

Lucy's Bar and Grille was an institution in Bay Point. It was no Sardis, the famed New York City restaurant with hundreds of celebs and Broadway stars on the walls, both in atmosphere or price, but it was charming nonetheless. Several black-and-white or color autographed celebrity photos hung on the walls, alongside old porcelain, Cajun art and other antique treasures her grandmother had brought with her from her native Louisiana.

To most people in Bay Point, her grandmother's restaurant was just a homespun place to eat, but Jasmine knew that it was Lucy's life. And she also knew that as the town continued to grow, so would the competition to threaten its existence.

"The men and the women were gorgeous. Glamorous! And the directors?" Lucy wrinkled her nose. "Pigs, mostly, with hands like an octopus."

She thought about her boss, Peter, and what he'd tried to do, what he wanted to do. A flash of anger rose up inside her, like bile, and Jasmine almost thought she was going to be sick. She poured herself a ginger ale and sipped it slowly until the feeling passed.

Donnie gathered up the last of the shiny aluminum carafes that held Lucy's famous "bottomless coffee." The lunch crowd was slowly filing out which meant only one thing. The dinner crowd would soon replace them, gathering again in the vintage button-tufted blue vinyl booths that lined the walls or at the green Formica tables scattered about the room.

Jasmine rang out the last customer at the bar and sighed. Since she'd arrived, she'd been so busy helping her grandmother that she barely had time to notice anything but receipts spitting out of a credit card machine, and the unpaid bills piling up in the back office.

Although Mayor Langston had done a great job revitalizing downtown Bay Point with new restaurants, housing and shops, and they had customers other than the regulars, they weren't out of the hole yet.

She'd already talked the landlord, George Stodwell, off the cliff of eviction. He'd given them another six months to pay the back rent owed or she'd be *selling jerk chicken from the trunk of her Mini Cooper.*

Jasmine wrung a rag out in the bar sink, wishing for a moment that it was Stodwell's neck. But she knew better than anyone that violence didn't solve anything. It just made things worse.

Besides, her grandmother needed her, though she

would never admit it. Now in her seventies, Lucy Dee Diller was as feisty and fierce as her Cajun dishes.

Growing up, Jasmine had never really known her. Lucy'd been so busy with the restaurant that she rarely returned to New Orleans. This was her chance to give her grandmother the love and affection she'd wanted to since she was a little girl. Lucy was trying to teach her how to cook, and now with her warning about Micah, also about men.

"Some guys are okay," Jasmine said, handing Lucy the cash drawer.

"Yes, the mayor is a fine man. But he's taken. Money and good looks flow throughout the Langston family tree, but as far as I'm concerned, Micah can plant his seed somewhere else."

"Lucy!" Jasmine croaked out a shocked laugh, as racy images flitted through her mind, but her grandmother had disappeared through the swinging doors into the kitchen.

Leaning her elbows on the bar, Jasmine felt her nipples tighten involuntarily as she recalled Micah's packed, athletic build. His white short-sleeved polo shirt and pressed khaki shorts, with just enough bulge in all the right places, and none of the wrong ones.

She licked her lips and drank the rest of her ginger ale to cool off.

Lucy reemerged and Jasmine crossed her arms over her chest.

"What are you standing around for?" Lucy called out, as she went to the front door and locked it. "Time to prep for dinner."

Jasmine slipped under the counter, rather than lift it up. “I’m on it.”

“Whew, girl,” Lucy said, walking back. “You make me nervous every time you do that.”

“I’m ok. Besides it’s good for my thighs.”

“Honey, I can’t even remember a time when I was able to squat that low.”

She gave Lucy a hug. “Why don’t you go up to your room and rest? Donnie, Gloria and I will handle prep.”

Every dish at Lucy’s Bar and Grille was made from fresh ingredients. Even the spices were freshly ground just before use.

“I guess you’re right. I could use a little nap.” Lucy wiped her brow. “I hope I’m not keeping you from whatever it is you kids do these days. I love having you here, but—”

“And I love being here,” Jasmine interrupted. “We’ve got a lot of missed time to make up for, don’t we?”

“We certainly do, and I’m treasuring every moment.”

Jasmine backed against one of the swinging doors to hold it open so her grandmother could pass. At the end of the kitchen, which smelled of roasted chicken, allspice and thyme, there was a short hallway with stairs that led up to a small apartment, which she shared with Lucy.

Although Jasmine had a fair amount of money in her savings account, she wanted to take her time to find her own place. She was hoarding her tips to get her stuff out of storage, when the time came. For her, Bay Point was not only a place to reconnect with her grandmother. She hoped it would be a refuge.

After she got Lucy settled upstairs, she went back down and started to cut onions, while Gloria sliced the potatoes. She was almost finished when Donnie informed her she had a call.

She swung into the main dining area and picked up the cordless at the hostess station. "Lucy's. This is Jasmine Kennedy. How can I help you?"

"Miss Kennedy. That sounds so presidential."

The man's low baritone voice, sounding vaguely familiar, sent a chill up her spine.

"Who is this?" she demanded in a sharp voice.

Donnie stopped stacking the highball glasses and frowned.

"Micah Langston."

"Oh," she said, letting Donnie know with a nod that everything was okay.

"Forget me so soon? I haven't forgotten about you."

Now that she knew who he was, his intimate insinuation transformed the chill in her spine into a pool of heat in her belly.

She sank onto a bar stool, not expecting to hear from him so soon, or even at all.

"What can I do for you, Micah?"

"I think I left my pen, a black Mont Blanc, very expensive, there at the bar. Can you check for me?"

Jasmine furrowed her brow. Pharmaceutical sales reps, who had Bay Point Community Hospital in their territories, often stopped in for breakfast or lunch on the way in or out of town. She distinctly remembered giving Micah a pen imprinted with the brand name of some kind of drug, but she'd humor the man. Besides, where would he have kept it? The polo shirt he'd worn had no pockets.

"Sure, hold on," she said, and set the phone upright on the bar.

Just for kicks, she did check near where he sat, but there was nothing but some food scraps on the floor. Not from him, she knew, but from the previous customer who routinely dropped food in his lap, while talking to his coworker.

"I'm sorry, but there's nothing here."

"Ah, but that's where you're wrong."

She narrowed her eyes. "What are you talking about?"

"You do have what I'm seeking. You just don't know it yet."

He sighed and the low sound vibrated, soft and sexy, against her ear as though he were right next to her.

Suddenly she knew what he was implying and her loins pulsed with need. And though he'd made her go chasing for something that didn't exist, she found him very exciting.

She sucked in a breath, and he chuckled softly.

"Get lost, Micah," she said, disconnecting the call.

Jasmine stuck her hands in her apron and brought out his receipt. She examined his signature, or autograph she supposed, if she were a fan, which she most definitely was not. Her eyes traced his phone number, committing it to memory.

Time for a fling? Perhaps.

Time for love? Not a chance.

Chapter 2

Micah chuckled as he pulled up to his parents' beachfront estate. With Jasmine's sexy New Orleans drawl still in his ear, his body hummed with desire. Even though she'd hung up on him, the call energized him.

Coming home always brought back the guilt that he'd left in the first place.

His parents were never happy with his decision to stay away from Bay Point after culinary school. Because of their deep roots in the community, they'd wanted him to start a business there, but he'd refused and his relationship with them had suffered.

It was important to him to make his own way, with or without their blessing. That feeling hadn't changed, although sometimes he wished things could have been different between them.

The briny ocean breeze hit him as soon as he stepped out of his air-conditioned car. He got his suitcase from the back seat, relieved to see that there were no other vehicles in the area adjacent to the circular driveway.

His brothers, Gregory and Marlon, always parked their cars in the attached six-car garage on the other side of the Spanish-style home. His parents loved to entertain on a regular basis, but it looked like tonight would be a family-only affair.

Micah felt a pain in his gut knowing that after ten years as a successful chef and restaurant owner, his parents still didn't respect his choice of a career.

This time, I won't let them get to me.

The scent of sand and seaweed further boosted his positive mood as he wheeled his suitcase up the red brick path to the front door. He punched in the security code, went in and stowed his bag next to the curved staircase, just outside the expansive foyer.

He slipped off his shoes and peeked in the library, which his father also used as an office. It was empty, so he strode into the large living room. The floor-to-ceiling windows bathed the space in late afternoon light and he could see everyone had gathered outside.

Micah closed the patio door behind him and was soon enveloped in his mother's embrace.

"It's good to have you home, son."

"For a small woman, you pack some powerful hugs," Micah joked, giving her a tight squeeze back.

Helen Langston, only five feet tall, was a giant of philanthropy in Bay Point, raising thousands of dollars for causes she cared about. In her early sixties, her demeanor with her children was often cool and distant, but in public and at parties she always turned on the charm. Impeccably dressed, even when just relaxing at home, her short coppery-brown hair was always cut in the latest style.

"I've been saving them up for a while," she said, after releasing her grip.

Gregory, the middle Langston, was lounging on a chaise. He uncrossed his ankles but did not get up.

"You can thank me for getting him back in town. I'm the one trying to get him to open up a restaurant here."

Micah strolled over. "Lying down on the job again, Mayor? At least give me a proper greeting."

He picked up Gregory's legs and swung them out of the way so he could sit down, ignoring his brother's protests.

"Okay, but I'm warning you, if I shake your hand, it's a done deal."

Micah got the hint and stood, a wry smile on his face, knowing his brother was dead serious. "My partners and I bought the building, but as you already know, we haven't decided whose restaurant will be utilizing the space."

Marlon, the eldest brother, strode over and draped an arm around his shoulders. He gave him a gruff, but hearty squeeze that almost caused Micah to trip over his own feet.

"If Gregory's big tax breaks won't work, can I tempt you with one of my not-so-famous mango margaritas?"

"Made with farm-fresh, organic ingredients?"

"Don't ask, just drink," Marlon teased.

Micah reached around and punched his brother's right shoulder, a funny kind of "man hug" that was a tradition with them.

"Hangover coming right up."

Marlon walked to the wrought iron patio table and grabbed a pitcher.

Micah chuckled when he poured a healthy serving of the frosty beverage into a margarita glass.

"Leave the man alone," his father admonished. "Be glad he had the decency to grace us with his presence this time."

Theodore (Theo) Langston swirled his half-filled glass of scotch and water from his seat under the edge of the table's huge umbrella, setting himself apart from the family as usual. It occurred to Micah that he was somewhat like him, but in the next moment, he told himself that wasn't true.

His father, a well-known personal injury attorney had the kind of class and style that could never be duplicated even though he was sometimes accused of being an ambulance chaser, mostly by jealous peers who couldn't get, nor handle, his caseload. He dealt in slips and falls, auto accidents, medical malpractice and other injuries, for clients in Bay Point and surrounding cities in Northern California.

"Bad day at work, Dad?" Micah asked, dragging over a chair next to him. The harsh sound of iron on stone made everyone wince.

"Nah, the usual." Theo raised his glass before draining the contents. "Since your brother became the mayor two years ago, my business has tripled, but I'm not complaining."

He rubbed his stomach and turned to his mother. "When is dinner? I'm starving."

She consulted her bracelet wristwatch, a family heirloom. Even though Micah wasn't in to jewelry, the bone china face with tiny hands, surrounded in diamonds, always awed him. The elegance of the piece suited her perfectly.

"You know your father won't eat a minute earlier than six p.m."

Micah sighed. His family drove him crazy, but for the most part, they were normal. Still, he wasn't so sure he liked being back home.

He stared at the ornate balcony that wrapped around the entire second floor. Growing up, the view from his room had beckoned him. First as a child watching the clouds move and the sun peek out, like his toes from under the bed sheets. Then as an adult, the view of the sun meant heat and surfing and pretty girls, and if he was lucky, a lot of sex.

There was Delores, his first, at age fourteen. Three years older with a driver's license and a pierced tongue. Body shaped like one of his surfboards, small breasts, thin lips, she knew how to ride him. Whenever they made out, she had to tap him on the mouth to remind him to breathe again.

He wanted to breathe, soft and hot, with Jasmine, her accent curling his ear, her beautiful body cuddled against him. And then what?

I take off, he thought, *just like the others.*

Micah finished his margarita, his mind a whirl of thoughts as he fought again his desire for a woman he'd met only hours before.

He wouldn't end up like Gregory who'd taken the plunge and married nearly two years ago. Vanessa was a florist and sole owner of Blooms in Paradise, a flower shop close to City Hall. They'd been childhood playmates that made mud pies and swung swings together. Now they were making babies.

"Where are Vanessa and little Lily?"

"Our sweet pumpkin has a bit of the sniffles so Vanessa decided to stay home and play it safe," Gregory said.

Helen, who was delighted at having a grandchild, and a girl at that, frowned.

"She's barely six months old. A cold could be dangerous. Was she seen by a doctor?"

"Yes, the very best," Gregory replied. "Her grandfather."

Helen closed her eyes briefly. "Of course she'd be seen by Vanessa's father. He's still chief of emergency, isn't he?"

Gregory nodded. "Yes, and refuses to retire."

"Likely because he would find himself with a new job, as your full-time babysitter," Marlon drawled.

"Vanessa enjoys being at home," Gregory shot back in a peeved tone. "Jewel is always happy to help out on our date nights."

"She's a nice woman," Helen replied. "I'm glad you get along with your mother-in-law."

Gregory gave her a kiss on the cheek, teasing. “I’m glad she gets along with you.”

She turned away. “What’s that supposed to mean? I’m easy to talk to.”

“In a crowd, perhaps, but not at home,” Marlon said, knowing everyone agreed with him. “You can be moody, Mom.”

“Why do you think Dad has to have two drinks before dinner?” Micah piped in.

“No,” his father insisted, drawing out the word. “It’s because I like them.”

“Wrong, Theo.” Helen placed a hand on his arm. “You like your little scotch and waters because you like to be right, and sometimes, when your sons or I am around, you have to admit you’re wrong.”

Micah popped on his phone. “It’s six o’clock. Time to go inside and chow down. I want to stop by the restaurant space and check it out before it gets too dark.”

The family left the patio and went through the living room to the formal dining room where Ginny Binslow, the Langstons’ longtime personal chef, was about to serve dinner. Micah didn’t know exactly how old she was, but she was like a second mother to him.

“I cooked your favorites,” she said, brown eyes in a round face gleaming. “Roast pork, mashed potatoes, fresh green beans and apple pie.”

“Thanks, you’re a doll.” Micah greeted her warmly with a peck on each cheek. “And if you want to hightail it out of this place, you know who to call.”

Ginny was the one who introduced him to a love of cooking by letting him help her prepare the meals at a very young age. He made his first Thanksgiving turkey by age seven, and won his first baking contest at age ten. She'd inspired and encouraged him to become a chef, much to the dismay of Helen, who only set foot in the kitchen to get to the second wing of the estate.

"Stop trying to steal Ginny," Helen commanded, as they gathered around the large oak table.

Theo and Helen each sat at a head of the table, Gregory and Marlon on the side closest to the windows, and Micah opposite them. He felt like his two brothers were about to play good cop, bad cop, but at least he had a great view of the Pacific.

"Yeah, I'm hoping he'll steal the hearts of Bay Pointers with his fabulous food," Gregory said, accepting a platter of pork from Theo.

"If you need an architect, I know just the person. Liza Marbet. She designed the new cosmetic surgery clinic that opened six months ago. Her husband, Anthony owns it."

"They had a huge gala there to celebrate the grand opening," Gregory said. "Mom was in her element."

"Dr. Marbet is a brilliant plastic surgeon. Although I don't need their services, I did stop in to take a look," Helen said. "It's spa-like modern with clean lines and just enough oomph to make the space seem very personal."

"Sounds nice, but I've got to get clearance on some building permits before I think about design."

"I can take care of that, bro." Gregory said. "Whatever you need."

Micah dug in to his mashed potatoes and thought a

moment before saying his next words. He didn't want to offend his brother, but he had to make a few things clear.

"Gregory, I just want to make sure that nobody in town finds out about this project."

His brother chewed, swallowed and stared at him. The other members of his family did the same.

"What's the big secret?" Theo barked, waving a fork in the air. "Any new restaurant is great for business downtown. Yours is sure to be an instant hit."

"More restaurants equal more competition, and some businesses can't handle that," Micah replied, surprised at his father's positive comment. Maybe he was slowly coming around to the fact that his son was happy being a chef.

"I think he's worried about generating buzz before any real decisions have been made," Marlon guessed. "At this point, all you've done is buy the building."

"Not me, personally," Micah corrected. "It was purchased by a shell company managed by my business partners in order to make it difficult to trace back to me, to protect my privacy. But you're right, I really need to keep a lid on this, and I'll need everyone's help."

"We won't tell a single living soul," Helen said, patting his hand as her eyes met those of her husband and sons. "The Langston's always stick together."

Marlon made a big show of twisting his fingers to his mouth and fake-throwing away the key. He yowled when Gregory nudged him in the ribs. Even though he was the oldest, sometimes he was the least serious.

"The nondisclosure agreement the city signed helps,

too," Gregory affirmed. "But of course the family won't breathe a word."

Micah thanked them, and they continued with the meal.

The sun had nearly set over the Pacific, rendering the sky in painted stripes of orange and pink over twilight blue.

He had second helpings while Gregory and Theo argued over political issues, both local and national. Helen and Marlon talked about the books they were reading. He stayed quiet, and found his thoughts turning to Jasmine.

After dinner, he begged off coffee and left to go back downtown to check out the interior space, which he'd only seen in photos. To avoid any possibility of being seen by Jasmine, he would park in the alley behind the building and enter through the back door.

On his way there, he thought about his family. How he wished he could tell them the real reason why they had to keep his secret.

That a woman he barely knew had made his heart race, and his body heat, and he was already worried.

About her. About him. About their future.

Jasmine splashed cold water on her face, hoping it would perk her up. She'd been on the clock for over fourteen hours. Her feet hurt, her clothes were sweaty and her mood was dark.

When she told her closest friends she was leaving New Orleans to work in her grandmother's restaurant, she'd laughed when they told her she was making a mistake.

She wasn't laughing now.

They were building successful careers in business, law and medicine, while she was building blisters between her toes.

She grabbed a paper towel and dried her hands. It was nights like these, of which there were many, that she questioned her decision, and others, like hanging up on Micah. Disappointment spiraled through her whenever she thought about not hearing from him again.

If he wants me, he'll call again, she assured herself.

Exiting the restroom, she stopped by the kitchen to make sure Lucy wasn't there. After closing out the dinner register, she'd asked her to go upstairs and relax, but her grandmother was always hesitant. She was woe to admit she wasn't as spry as she used to be.

Jasmine understood how hard it must be to let go of something she'd been doing for so many years. Her grandmother never said anything outright, but Jasmine could tell by the worry in her eyes that she was concerned about the future of the bar and grille.

Donnie and Gloria called out their goodbyes. When they left, she shut off the lights, removed her apron and sank down into a chair.

With a yawn she didn't bother to cover, she trailed her hand listlessly across the café curtains, parting them, and looked outside. Night had fallen. The parking spaces were empty, giving her a clear view of the empty building across Magnolia Avenue.

She'd seen no work being done, at least on the outside, but there was brown paper on the windows so the inside of the space was hidden from view. Lucy said that the entire building used to be a grocery store, so the space was huge, and they often speculated what type of business might move in.

"It better not be another restaurant," she muttered, letting the curtain fall back into place.

Although if it was, she was the best person to meet the challenge to her grandmother's business. Her work at the agency on marketing strategies to identify and circumvent competition was one of the high points of her life and she was pretty good at it. Maybe she'd end up doing more for her grandmother than pouring beers and learning to cook.

Maybe she'd actually help Lucy save her business.

Jasmine decided to take a walk and clear her head before going to bed. After locking the front door, she glanced across the street and her breath caught in her throat.

A light swiveled inside the building, a muted glow like a flashlight under a sheet, intermittently and at different parts of the otherwise dark space. Before she knew what was happening, her feet began to move and she crossed Magnolia Avenue. Cupping her hands against the window glass, she peered in, not really expecting to see anything, and didn't.

"What's up, Jazzy?"

Jasmine spun on her sneakers, nostrils flaring, and was surprised to see Micah. She'd been so focused on trying to see the source of the light that she didn't even see him approach.

"W-what are you doing here?"

She couldn't stand it when folks called her "Jazzy" or worse, "Jaz," and thought it was a form of subtle disrespect. But out of Micah's mouth, it sounded sensual, like the flower for which she was named.

She looked left and right, disoriented to see him now, and so soon. The old-fashioned streetlights cast a yellowish glow on the sidewalk.

"Where did you come from?"

"My parents' beach house. After dinner, I decided to come back downtown and see if I can get into any trouble."

His eyes slid from her face all the way down her body, leaving jet-spurts of intense warmth she wanted to feel again.

She stepped closer, hand on her hip, wishing she'd changed out of her work clothes. He hadn't changed his outfit either and she almost burst out laughing when she realized they were both undressing each other with their eyes.

"What did you have in mind?"

"A ride." Her eyebrows shot up, until he thumbed backward. "On the Bay Point Carousel."

"Oh," she said, exhaling a slow breath.

"I detect a tone of disappointment, Miss Kennedy."

"Not at all. The Carousel is fun."

But not as much fun as riding on you would be, she thought, holding back a smile.

"Too bad it's already shut down for the night. Last ride is at eight thirty."

"Let's go for a stroll anyway. I have a feeling that we both need to clear our heads."

He crooked his right arm at the elbow. "Shall we?"

Jasmine ignored the gesture and walked away, knowing that if he touched her, she would find him even more difficult to resist. She told herself that the only reason she was heading east, and not going back across the street where she belonged, was because she was going to take a walk anyway.

"If you won't take my arm, will you at least take my advice?" he asked, catching up to her.

Jasmine shrugged. "Depends on what it is."

"Don't go peering into windows that are papered over. Chances are the owner doesn't want you to see what's in there."

She stopped in her tracks and stared up at him. "I was closing up the restaurant and thought I saw a light being waved around."

At his skeptical look, she paused. "At least I think I did."

"While you're snooping, someone else is dialing nine-one-one."

"I wasn't snooping," she insisted, poking him lightly in the chest. "Just like you didn't lose your pen."

He grinned. "The point goes to you. All I meant was that I would hate to have to bail you out of jail."

"You could call in a favor with the mayor."

"I could, if I knew you better."

"Is that why you came back tonight, and why you called to bug me earlier today?"

"What do you think?"

"I don't know. You just got home today. Any particular reason why you are back in town?"

"Just to relax and see my family." He shrugged.

Jasmine folded her arms. "And you want to get away from them so soon?"

"Do you want to be around your family twenty-four-seven?"

"My folks don't live on a palatial estate on the beach," she tossed back in a breezy tone.

"Where are they? Back in New Orleans, I presume?"

She nodded. "My mother is but by dad lives in Baton Rouge. They divorced when I was twelve."

As far as Jasmine was concerned, her grandmother was the only family she had right now.

He led her by the elbow to a bench near the carousel.

"I'd like to know more about you and Lucy."

She glanced down Magnolia Avenue toward the restaurant.

"Why? The only thing you need to know is that she relies on me, so I better get back."

He captured her hand, his touch gentle, but insistent.

"Stay with me a minute. Please?"

She paused for a moment, before sitting down.

"How do you like living in Bay Point so far?" he asked. "Complete opposite of New Orleans?"

She leaned back against the bench and nodded. "It's small, quiet at night, maybe too quiet. I like the people for the most part. I like running on the beach, and the breezes that smell of salt and sand. I feel safe here."

"Did something happen back in New Orleans?"

She swallowed hard, and wondered what he would think if she told him about her former boss.

"No, I just meant that there's not a lot of crime here. I guess because it's so small. I worry what will happen as the town continues to grow."

"The police force will grow with it," he said. "I know that Gregory is committed to continuing to bring new commerce into the town and more residents, but he's also focused on keeping everyone safe, too."

"That's good to know. I heard he doesn't want Bay Point to become a roadside tourist trap either."

"I agree with him." Micah crossed his legs at the ankles. "We're close enough to the Pacific Coast Highway to be easily accessible, but not so close to have any drive-through restaurants. If people want to eat here, they have to park and get out of their cars."

"Yes, people do tend to shop or check out the rest of the town, either before or after they eat."

As the minutes passed, their conversation remained on the town. Micah, who claimed to be a local history buff, relayed some little-known stories that Jasmine found amusing, but far-fetched. She had a feeling that it would be easy for them to converse back and forth for hours on end.

"Tell me something. Why go through the trouble of getting to know me when you're only just visiting for a few days?" she posed.

"That doesn't mean we have to be strangers, does it?"

"I suppose we can start out as casual acquaintances," Jasmine replied, giving in a little because she wanted to continue to see him.

"I don't have a problem with that, if you promise to have dinner with me before I go."

She pursed her lips. "I'm not sure I can spare the time. I work at the restaurant pretty much from sunup to sundown."

"Doesn't Lucy ever give you a break?"

"She's the one who works too hard," Jasmine said in her grandmother's defense.

"Then I'll just have to charm her into giving you a night off."

"Ha! Give it a try, but she's no fool, Micah. She told me all the Langston men were flirts."

"And do you believe her?"

Jasmine folded her arms. "I'm still waiting for you to prove her right."

Micah grinned. "Are you challenging me?"

"What do you think?"

He gave her a wide grin. "I think I like you. You're beautiful, funny and—"

"Leaving," she interrupted and stood, heart hammering in her chest.

Micah frowned. "Why so soon?"

"I've been away too long. I better go see if Lucy is okay."

Living with her grandmother was a little like living with her parents, no privacy until after they were asleep. She couldn't wait until she could get her own place.

"I'll go with you."

"No, I'd rather be alone right now. See you later."

Jasmine walked away, feeling his eyes on her back.

It took everything in her power to keep on going. When she got to the restaurant, she turned around and the park bench was empty.

Micah circled around City Hall, before heading back to the alley. Back in his car, he breathed a sigh of relief.

"That was too close," he muttered and realized that keeping his restaurant a secret was going to be very stressful.

After he'd emerged from the alley next to Vanessa's flower shop, which was seven stores down from his space, and saw Jasmine trying to peek into the windows, he'd hesitated even approaching her. But he had to find out what she'd seen, or even better, what she'd been doing.

She'd taken him totally by surprise.

Although she'd claimed she was only taking a walk, Micah was afraid that she'd already caught the "snooping bug," which many residents seemed to have in spades. They were intelligent, inquisitive and never could seem to find the time to mind their own business.

Maisie Barnell, owner of the only bed-and-breakfast establishment in town, was known as the eyes and ears of Bay Point, but she did it because she cared about its people.

Micah twisted his lips, realizing that tonight at least, he was being somewhat of a snoop himself. At first, his whole point of inviting her to the carousel park was to distract her. He wanted to talk to her enough to make her forget whatever she saw even if it was only the light from his phone.

Later, as they began to talk, he wanted to learn more about her. When she talked about New Orleans, her tone sounded nostalgic, but he also caught a hint of fear when he asked if something bad had happened to her.

When she denied it, he sensed she was lying. Out of respect, he didn't question her further, but he'd felt a surge of tenderness for her, wanting her to feel safe, no matter where she happened to be. Hoping that she felt at ease with him.

He felt confident she didn't suspect him as the "intruder" or that she even saw anything at all. Still, he decided that he would call the contractor and have him triple the paper on the windows. He wasn't going to take any chances of anyone in Bay Point finding out that he was part owner of the space.

He wanted to see Jasmine again. Not to cover his tracks, but to really get to know her this time. She'd been glib about his dinner invite, even though he was serious.

He knew firsthand that working in the restaurant business left very little time for a real relationship. Closing his eyes, he recalled hot and heavy trysts in supply closets, vacant hotel rooms in-between guest check-ins, even alleys like the ones behind his restaurant.

That's not what he wanted with Jasmine.

He was eager to get back to his parents' house and be alone in his room. He wanted to think about Jasmine, the glow of her skin under the streetlamps, and how the light cast shadows in the swell of her cleavage.

There was something about Jasmine that made him think she could be the woman who could finally make him set down roots, though not necessarily in Bay Point. He wanted her badly, but he had to move slowly. With so much at stake for both of them, he wasn't sure it would be fair to take the chance, no matter where it would lead.

Chapter 3

Jasmine flipped the closed sign on the front door. Today was the annual Bay Point Bake-off, and apparently, it was a really big deal. For over thirty years, the event had been held at Bay Point Baptist Church. This year, the committee decided to move to Carousel Park, hoping the centralized location would help boost attendance.

Lucy had participated with one of her recipes for many years, but had never won anything except honorable mentions. She'd also been a judge. Several days ago, she'd fallen ill with a bad cold, and was too sick to work, let alone go anywhere outside of the apartment.

The bake-off had to be important for Lucy to close the restaurant early. Jasmine had told her grandmother that she could help Gloria cook, so they could remain open, instead of attending the bake-off. The event had been publicized on social media, and they were expecting a large crowd downtown.

But Lucy had refused, telling her that they all needed a break. Even though she knew she would be losing out on tourist dollars that day, she felt it was important that the restaurant was represented, not only in the bake-off, but also in the bake sale that took place immediately afterward. All proceeds from both events were donated to charity.

On her first night in town, Jasmine was looking for a blanket in Lucy's linen closet and found an old wooden cigar box in the back. She'd taken it back to her room, opened it and spent a few hours perusing the contents, which was a collection of recipes, while her grandmother slept.

In the morning, Lucy told her that they belonged to her mother, Melba Louise Kennedy, Jasmine's great-grandmother. Jasmine was surprised to learn that Lucy's famous jerk chicken recipe was passed down to her from Melba, but not in written form.

Lucy encouraged her to try making some of her great-grandmother's recipes.At first, Jasmine balked at her suggestion. She was having enough difficulty trying to learn how to cook Lucy's recipes.

She gave in when Lucy said that maybe they could add one or more to the restaurant menu. She knew it was important for a restaurant to change things up every once in a while, with new appetizers, entrees, sides or desserts. None of the recipes in the box had been made in years, and Jasmine was hopeful that one of them would be able to lift Lucy's Bar and Grille from relative obscurity among tourists to must-visit status.

In preparation for the bake-off, she'd spent weeks after-hours baking a variety of New Orleans treats, from beignets to croissants to madeleines before settling on her great-grandmother Melba's pie recipe.

Jasmine placed her entry, a triple berry crumb crust pie carefully in a white box. She'd baked a second pie for the sale and boxed that one up, too. Then she tied a red ribbon on top of both. When she was finished, she took a step back and smiled with satisfaction. Out of everything she'd baked recently, the pies were her favorite and she was looking forward to making more.

She heard the creak of old floorboards, and glanced up at the ceiling. Lucy's bedroom was directly over the kitchen. Jasmine knew that Lucy drew strength from all the wonderful smells that managed to creep into the apartment from below.

Her grandmother was in relatively good health, but standing on her feet from dusk to dawn for so many years had taken its toll. She tired easily and had lower back issues that could require surgery if the condition worsened. Thick-soled orthopedic shoes helped, but only for a few hours and then she had to go upstairs and rest.

She wished they could hire another cook to help Gloria, but Lucy said she didn't have the money to hire new workers. Plus, many of the locals were attracted to the newer restaurants coming to town that often promised higher wages, tips and better health benefits.

As a marketing professional, Jasmine knew advertising was expensive, but word-of-mouth was free and the most trusted among customers. Her grandmother had worked too hard, and too long to lose her rightful place among Bay Point's original small businesses. Today, she would set in motion her plan to help solidify the future of Lucy's Bar and Grille.

After checking in on Lucy, who was fast asleep, she went back downstairs and picked up the pie boxes.

On her way out, she glanced across the street as she headed toward Carousel Park. She hadn't dared to peek inside the building again, even though, day after day, her curiosity grew. No work had been done on the exterior of the building, although she did see a couple of contractors up on the roof several days ago.

But she hadn't heard from Micah, nor had he stopped in, and it surprised her how much that bothered her.

The day after their conversation, she felt she was walking a tightrope of suspense. Waiting for him to come in for breakfast, then for lunch. When he didn't show for either, she held out some hope for dinner, but all she got was disappointment.

She'd enjoyed their conversation immensely, yet the whole experience had shaken her up a bit. It scared her that she was so intent on finding out what was going on in the space that she hadn't noticed him walking up behind her.

The same thing had happened at her job, except she was sitting at a table, completely focused on a task, unaware that her boss who was next to her, was slowly reaching his hand under the table to paw at her thigh.

Jasmine shuddered at the memory. Her reasons for

peeking into the building were completely innocent, but she wondered what Micah really thought about her.

Perhaps he'd gotten called out of town, she reasoned to herself. She'd neglected to ask him how often he came back because she didn't want to appear too nosy. Most of all, she regretted not accepting his dinner invite in the first place. This time, playing it coy had backfired big time. Making the final tweaks to her recipe the rest of the week had helped to keep him off her mind for the most part, but he still lurked there, making her yearn to be in his presence.

Would she ever see him again?

She tripped on a raised crack in the sidewalk and yelped, almost losing her precious pies and her dignity. Thank goodness no one seemed to notice. She decided not to spend one more second thinking about a man who could make her lose her heart just as easily.

Cars jostled for the few remaining parking spaces on Ocean Avenue, and she could see that the ones that jutted out like spokes on a bicycle wheel in front of the carousel were filled.

The line to ride the carousel was long and filled with smiling children and adults. She waved to Mariella Vency, who was manning the little wooden ticket booth, painted periwinkle blue.

Mariella worked at City Hall in the mayor's office, but Jasmine wasn't clear on her role. She would often call the restaurant and order a big platter of sandwiches, cole slaw and assorted sodas for meetings. Jasmine smiled and wondered how many decisions, both good and bad, were made while consuming her grandmother's delicious food.

She rounded the carousel, greeting some familiar faces along the way and arrived at the main gazebo a few minutes later.

"Hey Maisie!" she called, going up the stairs.

"Hello, Jasmine. Where's Lucy? Is she feeling better?"

Jasmine frowned inwardly, wondering how Maisie knew her grandmother was challenged with health issues, but she supposed word got around town. Lucy was under the impression that everyone thought she made every meal personally. Maybe she had when she first started the restaurant, but not anymore.

"She's not feeling well today, so I'm here in her place."

"I'm so sorry to hear that, but it's best that she stay home and rest. Lucy is quite a mainstay at this event and I hope she'll feel better soon."

Jasmine set the pies down on the table. "Thanks, I'll tell her."

"Are you entering both of those in the bake-off?"

"No, just one. The other is for the bake sale."

Maisie nodded and handed her a form and a pen. "Fill this out and you're all set."

Jasmine wrote down her name and cell phone number on the paper. "I've never entered a bake-off contest. How does it work?"

"You haven't? Oh my dear, you are in for a treat, no pun intended." Maisie laughed, clasping her hands together. "The first thing you need to know is that the contest is double-blind."

"What does that mean?"

Maisie leaned closer to the table. "The judges won't know who made the recipe. That's to avoid any potential conflicts of interest. Whether a person wins or loses, the baker will never know who judged their entry. Even I won't have that information," she finished with a sniff, as if she were offended.

Maisie cut two numbers from a sheet of paper. She slipped one in the first pie box and handed the other number to Jasmine.

"Keep this somewhere safe, and don't display it on your person. At the end of the afternoon, you'll know if you've won something when they call your number and name."

Jasmine nodded and stuck the paper in the back pocket of her shorts. She watched as Maisie set her pie box on a long table filled with other competitor's treats.

"What about this pie?"

"Take it inside, to the rotunda and set it on the table there."

She picked up the second pie box. "I'm so nervous."

Maisie gave her a smile. "Honestly, so am I. Normally, this is a very casual event, but everyone is on pins and needles this year. Not because of who has entered, but who will be judging."

Jasmine arched a brow. "I thought it was just women from the church who are part of the event committee."

"No, this year we are joined by a very special, and very handsome, I might add, celebrity guest."

Though she had no idea who it was, Jasmine felt her heart begin to squeeze in her chest.

"And who might that be?"

Maisie glanced around, before motioning Jasmine with her index finger, to lean over the table. She could hardly contain her excitement.

"Chef Micah Langston. Can you believe it?"

Hearing his name from someone else's lips made her heart beat faster, and then drop just as quick. The carnival music in the air seemed to collapse around her in a hellish heap of offbeat notes.

She said goodbye to Maisie and as she walked down the gazebo steps toward City Hall, her feet felt like they were molded of lead.

The knowledge that he was in town and had never stopped into the restaurant left her more confused than ever. Nothing like being rejected out right and not even knowing it, but Jasmine decided she wouldn't let him ruin her day. The one thousand dollar grand prize would go a long way toward helping her save for her own place, and she intended to emerge the winner.

"What was I thinking when I signed up for this?"

Micah ignored the shocked, openmouthed stares of the other bake-off judges in the room, none of whom he knew by name. What were they going to do? Fire him? He was the one who'd made the mistake of accepting the event in the first place.

Besides, he was a celebrity, not that he would ever pull rank. This was just another favor for Gregory gone wrong. Maybe he should take this as a clue and get the heck out of Bay Point.

He leaned back, hands folded across his stomach.

"Obviously, I wasn't thinking at all," he muttered, earning a few more side-eyes.

While some of his fellow compadres only had what seemed like a fingernail scratch of their individual serving, he had to take enough of a taste to get the full flavor, otherwise, he knew he'd be doing the cook a disservice.

It was a good thing he didn't know who made the desserts, some of which were positively atrocious and almost unpalatable. A few times he had to restrain himself from blurting out that a particular dish was not fit for human consumption. Judges were forbidden from talking out loud or amongst each other during the judging process.

He leaned back more in his chair, a little too far and managed to grab the edge of the table just in time. Righting himself, he grabbed his head with both hands, swooning because he was so dizzy.

Prentice, the City Hall security guard peeked his head into the room, where for the last ninety minutes, he'd been wheeling a cart filled with entries for the judges to sample.

"You'll be glad to hear that last batch was the last of 'em, judges!"

Micah stood up so fast that his chair crashed to the floor and pointed to him. "That man, ladies and gentlemen, deserves a round of applause."

The stern atmosphere in the room disappeared and

everyone broke out into smiles and cheers. Maisie hip-bumped Prentice out of the way and entered the room.

"We're not done yet, gang. Please give me your sheets so I can tally the scores." She gathered the paperwork from all the judges. "Micah, you will be handing out the awards, so please meet me at the gazebo in about twenty minutes. Everyone else is invited to stick around to see who our lucky winners are this year. Thank you so much for judging our contest!"

Micah sat down and remained as still as a bullfrog on a rock. He didn't even move when the floor was swept and the table was folded up in front of him. Finally, Prentice needed to put his chair away so he was forced to get up.

He placed the chair in the rollaway cart with the others. "I feel the same way you do every Sunday night, when Maisie practically forces another helping of mashed potatoes down my throat. That woman can't take no for an answer!"

"What we do for our girls, eh?" Micah commented.

"You want my advice? Stay single."

Micah laughed and checked his phone. It was time for the awards presentation.

There was a large crowd gathered when he arrived at the gazebo. Gregory was at the podium about to make an announcement. He jogged up to the stairs to a scattering of enthusiastic applause and put one hand over the microphone.

"Bro, you owe me big time."

"What are you—"

Gregory stopped when Micah stepped away from the

podium, a huge smile on his face. He shook his head and adjusted the mic back into position.

"Ladies and gentlemen. We are about to announce the lucky winners of the twenty-fifth annual Bay Point Bake-off Competition!" He waited until the cheers died down. "But first, I would like to introduce you to our celebrity judge, host of *High Stakes Chef* and my little brother, Micah Langston!"

Micah stepped to the edge of the platform and bowed.

Gregory glanced around. "Can I have the envelope, please?"

Maisie emerged from the side of the crowd, raising her arm, and waving the envelope in the air. "Here it is, Mayor! Sorry, I had to double-check my math."

Gregory reached down and took it from her. "Thank you, Maisie." He glanced over his shoulder. "Micah, you'll find the ribbons on the table just behind me."

All of the awards, except one, were honorable mentions, and none had names on them. All he had to do was hand them out, but he must have been too slow because by the time he turned around, there was a line of women, and a few men, snaking up the stairs of the gazebo. He gave each of them a smile, a nod and a ribbon as they passed by.

"And last but not least, for her Triple Berry Crumb Crust Pie, the grand prize winner is number 17… Jasmine Kennedy!"

The crowd erupted in applause. Micah heard a few people say "who?" Others craned their heads around in confusion. But he was the most confused of all.

Moments later, she stepped up to the platform. He

gave her a smile and slipped the large, blue-ribboned medal around her slender neck.

"I didn't know you baked."

"I didn't know you were still in town."

Then he gave her something he hadn't given anyone else. A kiss on the cheek.

Though the gesture was polite on the outside, he felt his heart hammer with desire. The electricity of attraction between them was palpable, and he briefly wondered if anyone in the audience had noticed.

"Disappointed I didn't stop by?"

She grabbed the medal and held it up. "Not anymore."

Before he could say anything, Gregory pulled them aside for a photo op for the *Bay Point Courier.* A crowd swarmed around him waving pens and phones, and out of the corner of his eye, Micah saw Jasmine back away.

He shook hands, signed autographs and took selfies. By the time he was finished, she was long gone and he knew he wasn't going to let her get away again. So he did the only thing he could do. He took his phone out of his pocket and called her.

"We need to talk."

At the sound of Micah's sexy voice, Jasmine's breath caught in her throat. She hadn't expected to hear from him, but she couldn't deny their chemistry when he slipped the medal around her neck. It was a moment before she could respond.

"I feel like we've talked enough."

Her thumb was on the end call button when she heard him shout through the phone. "Don't hang up, please!"

"Why shouldn't I?"

"Because I have an additional prize that you won, besides being Best in Show."

Jasmine narrowed her eyes, immediately suspicious. "I know I've won a thousand dollars, which is awesome enough. Are you telling me there's something else?"

"Yes, there is. Meet me at the pier in half an hour and I'll give you more details."

The line went dead. Her lips lifted at the corners, and she couldn't help but be intrigued.

What was the man up to now?

She put her phone on the bureau and glanced up in the mirror. She felt grimy all over from being around the crowds at the bake-off. If she hurried, she could take a quick shower and change.

Lucy was awake when she got home, and was overjoyed when she showed her the award. Afterward, she brought her into the living room, heated some soup and put on Lucy's favorite television program. Jasmine checked in on her again, and then continued down the hallway to the bathroom.

Hot water pattered on her shower cap as she lathered her body with her favorite lilac-scented soap. She tried to think of reasons why she should not meet Micah.

Other than the fact that he could break her heart, there were none. Curiosity had trampled her fears. She wanted to hear what he had to say, and at that moment, was confident she would be able to resist his advances.

She dried off and slathered on some body oil. Back

in her room, she selected her favorite sundress. It was cherry red, hit about midthigh and had a corset bodice, so no bra was required. Arranging her hair so her short cut had just enough spike, she slipped on a pair of pink pearl drop earrings and was ready to go.

She walked into the living room in her silver flip-flops. “Lucy, I’m going down to the pier for a little while. Will you be okay?”

Her grandmother put down a magazine and smiled. “You look beautiful. I’ll be fine. When you come back, we’ll have a little talk.”

Once outside, Jasmine shook her head at Lucy’s cryptic comment, wondering what she might want to discuss. Though she’d never talked about selling the restaurant, Jasmine often wondered what her plans were, once they got out of debt. Would she retire here or back in her native Louisiana?

The beach was about ten minutes walking distance from downtown. She made her way down the steep stairs built into the side of the cliff.

Walking barefoot now, she spotted Micah waiting for her on the pier. Though she couldn’t see his eyes, she could feel them on her body. Enjoying the heat from the afternoon sun and the feel of the sand squishing through her toes, she deliberately slowed her pace so he could take a nice, long look.

A few minutes later, she reached the pier, and waited until she was right in front of him to wriggle her red-painted toes into her flip-flops.

He was dressed in a white cotton shirt, half-unbuttoned in the heat, giving her a slivered preview of his hairless chest. His sky blue chino shorts accentuated his muscular thighs and rounded ass.

The waves slapped against the pier and seagulls cackled in the sky above them, but the noises faded into the background. Some people were fishing; others were scattered about sitting on benches and talking. No one was really near them so she felt like they were totally alone.

Though she was surrounded on three sides by water, her throat and lips felt dry as toast. Micah's body was an open call to a good time. He was the most gorgeous man she'd seen in a very long time, and the first she wanted to immediately sleep with, just based on his looks alone. If it was night, and they were alone, she would fall into his arms willingly.

Yet, she had to be careful. Though he never promised to call her, he'd already proven himself unreliable. *What can you expect from a celebrity,* she thought as he took her hand.

Before she could say anything, he ran one finger down the side of her neck, stopping just above her collarbone.

"Where's your medal?"

She shivered. "I left it at home," she said, her voice shaking a little. "Lucy was so proud of me, says she's going to display it near the bar."

"It looks way prettier on you." He whistled low, and the sound curled in her ear like a song. "You look gorgeous. Going to a party?"

"You made it seem on the phone like I had more to celebrate."

He took her other hand and held it. “Indeed you do, and you’ll be wise to accept it.”

“I’d like to know what it is first,” she said, wetting her lower lip with her tongue, well aware that his eyes were tracing her movements.

“A private cooking class with me at a local winery owned by a buddy.”

Jasmine raised a brow. “I never saw that on the original entry form.”

“Nor did you see my name as a judge.”

She gave him a little smile. “How did you happen to be there?”

“My brother called in another favor. I guess he’s paying me back for stealing all his favorite toys when we were kids. At first, I was pissed at him for getting me into it, until you walked up on stage.”

She hitched in a breath as he pulled her closer to him and she felt her nipples tighten against the bodice of her dress.

“It’s a good thing I didn’t know you were a judge. I never would have entered.”

“Why not? You deserved that award.”

“Because of who you are. I would have been very intimidated had I known.”

“The better for both of us that you didn’t then.”

Caw-caw! Caw-caw!

They both looked up at the same time as a seagull swooped down a little too close to their heads. She gasped and Micah clutched her body to his. He waved one hand in the air to frighten the bird away.

When it was gone, he didn’t let go, and she didn’t

want him to. She was finally where she wanted to be, ever since he'd set foot in her grandmother's restaurant.

She laid her cheek on his chest and inhaled. If he wore cologne, it was very lightly applied, which was fine with her. She preferred the scent of clean skin, as opposed to scents splashed from a bottle.

"That was scary," she whispered, looping her arms around his waist. "But this feels nice."

Enclosed between his strong arms and with her head nestled against his muscular chest, she did not feel confined. She felt empowered, free to say what she felt in her heart.

Micah placed his palms on her cheeks and stared into her eyes. He closed his eyes and brought his lips to hers.

"I'll bet this will feel even better."

His kiss was sweet and tender, and she felt her body melt against his.

He lifted his mouth briefly and sighed, his breath warm against her lips. She held back a gasp at how deliciously hard he felt against her belly. She pressed closer as his fingers caressed her cheeks.

"Hmm...that was a good start," she murmured.

He leaned against the railing. "I take it you want some more, Miss Kennedy?"

She gazed up at him, with half-lidded eyes and a seductive smile. "What do you think?"

He tightened his grip on her waist, and turned her around, so his back was to the other people on the pier.

"Just a little?"

His voice was low and thick, and sent a tingle down her spine.

"Maybe a lot," she admitted. A pang of desire hit her so strongly that it nearly took her breath away.

"Happy to oblige."

He caught her lips quickly in his, as if he didn't want to take the chance of refusal. The soft, roaming pressure of his mouth on hers had a kind of urgency that could overtake her senses, if she let it.

And she did. Gladly welcoming his lips, tasting his tongue with hers as their kisses widened and morphed, consuming them both.

Micah broke the kiss suddenly and looked back over his shoulder quickly. It occurred to her that he was double-checking that no one was around them. Though he wanted her, and she wanted him, she appreciated his concern for their privacy.

Then his lips took hers again, as if he'd never paused, creating a heat uniquely their own. As his kiss deepened, he brought his hand slowly down her bodice and cupped her right breast. Her own kisses became insistent, driven by his fingers, roaming and gently kneading her imprisoned flesh.

Micah grunted low and rested his elbow on the wooden railing, angling her slightly, allowing his fingers to explore in a more comfortable position. She sucked on his bottom lip and moaned softly while he massaged and tweaked her nipple with his thumb until it was painfully stiff under her clothes.

She broke away, panting as the pressure of his maleness, hidden and hard against her dress, made her want to hitch up her dress and mount him right there. It took all of her will not to rub her abdomen against his penis, as her hands clutched at the nape of his neck, as his tongue licked at her earlobe.

It was sweet and sexy, a little bit naughty, kissing a man she barely knew, but one that she wanted so badly. His hips began to move, every so slowly against her, fluid and sensual, so that only she could detect it. The lust he was feeling at the moment, he was feeling only for her.

And at that moment, she didn't care if she ever got his heart, all she wanted was him.

He caught her lips back in his and the wind stole her moan and whipped through her legs. Her skirt billowed out and she wished he would duck his head underneath, and put his mouth and fingers on her sex.

Then his kisses became lighter, though he was breathing hard. She threw her hands around his neck and drew him closer, not wanting to take a chance that he'd leave her again. She wasn't done with him yet. She wanted more.

To her surprise, he suddenly pulled away, leaving her loins pulsing painfully with disappointment. She glanced over at the waves crashing on the sand and bit her lower lip to stem the dizziness in her head and to remember how he tasted, before that, too, disappeared.

"You call that a little?" she challenged.

Micah tipped her chin up, and gave her a peck on the nose. "No. I call that just an appetizer."

Jasmine pulled away, still aroused and ran her hands down her bodice, smoothing it over her taut nipples.

She wanted him, not his teasing. Couldn't he see that?

His eyes roamed over her body, watching her. With

a smile on his lips, he made some adjustments of his own, and her eyes dropped to his waist. The bulge she saw in his pants was going to keep her up at night.

He leaned his elbows back on the railing, his stance casual, as if what had just happened between them hadn't occurred at all.

"So…how about it? Think you're ready for a private lesson with me?"

Jasmine stared at him, ignoring the thrill that the sound of his voice gave her, and folded her arms at her chest.

"Can you promise me we'll only be cooking?"

He folded his arms and gave her a wicked grin. "Can you promise me we won't?"

Micah Langston had teased her to distraction for the very last time. She huffed out a deep breath, took a step towards him and slipped out of her flip-flops. She stuck one under her arm and threw the other one at him, and then calmly walked down the pier and onto the beach.

Chapter 4

Micah propped his feet up on the iron railing outside his room and stared into the distance. Early morning clouds stretched like white rubber bands across the sky, blocking the sun. The waves beckoned him to come down to the beach and play, but he had work to do, and decisions to make.

He picked up the silver flip-flop that Jasmine had thrown at him and laid it across his knee. He traced the crystal bling on top with his fingers, and his movements reminded him of touching her curvy, shapely body. He started to get hard and stopped, slapping the shoe against the side of his leg to distract himself.

She was a barefooted princess, and he was a flat-footed prince. The passion behind her kisses had surprised him, and he wanted more of them. He didn't know what to say or do next. It had been over a week since they'd met at the pier, and he hadn't called her or visited.

Back to business. That was always his excuse when he started to care about a woman. Working hard was easier than working on a relationship. The problem was, since he met Jasmine, he knew his priorities were all wrong, but he wasn't willing to change. No matter how sexy she was or how much he wanted her. He didn't even know where to start, so why start at all?

"I'm still weighing all my options," he told his business partners, Gary and Todd, who were based in New York. "If you push me for an answer now, it won't be the one that you want."

Including not opening a restaurant at all.

Micah heard Gary sigh loud and clear through the speakerphone.

"We're running out of time, Micah."

"We've got to start the design phase soon," Todd exclaimed. "Or else we won't stay on track."

"We're all doing well financially," Gary said. "But you're the one on television, not us."

Todd added, "Opening up *your* restaurant in *your* hometown, a little-known celebrity haven that is back on the upswing. It's a slam dunk!"

"I know guys, but there's still some things I need to work out," Micah said. "There's an architect in town I'd like us to meet who comes highly recommended. It's really important to my brother that we hire locally as much as possible. We can add her pitch to the others who've already submitted, and then review all of them together before coming to a final decision."

After a few more minutes of haggling, Micah told his partners that he'd contact them in a couple of days.

He ended the call, let out a deep breath and slung his arms behind his head. Sometimes he got tired of being asked his opinion. He just wanted everything good to happen with his business, as if by magic, rather than consensus. But everything hinged on his ability to move quickly and decisively. With his business and his love life.

He wanted to take his time with Jasmine, get to know her, uncover little things about her personality that maybe she wasn't even aware of, then make love to her nice and slow.

But he wasn't sure if he should take the risk. If she found out he was building a restaurant that could have a negative impact on Lucy's business, she would hate him. Lucy would hate him. The entire population of Bay Point might hate him.

His survival of the fittest mentality had always cast aside the future survival of a relationship with any women. He had to take the same attitude with Jasmine. He was in Bay Point to make money. End of story.

But that red dress! He groaned and threw his head back against his lounge chair, remembering how Jasmine looked in it, how she felt in it and how much he wanted to tear it off her. He saw her beautiful face, imagined the soft curves of her cheeks. Ever since that day, his body felt agitated and jumpy with unfulfilled desire.

He wasn't used to his advances being rejected, and there was no way he was going to stand for it, especially when it was clear that she wanted him as much as he wanted her.

"Trouble in paradise?"

"I think he's asleep."

Micah sat up with a growl and brushed the ice cubes off his bare chest, as his feet thudded on the concrete.

He glared at his two brothers, both smiling like Christmas elves. "What is this? An ambush?"

"It's certainly not an intervention," Gregory said, toeing the ice cubes under the railing and off the second floor porch.

"At least, not yet," Marlon grinned, handing him a dark pink drink in a champagne flute. "Try it. It's my version of a pomegranate mimosa."

Micah took a sip and gagged. "What's in this? Cough syrup?"

"Just a little brandy, infused with chili peppers. The first sip will give you a kick, but the next one will send you flying."

Micah made a face, and handed it back to him. "I love you bro, but no."

Marlon shrugged. "Back to the drawing board. I'll see you guys for breakfast."

"You sly fox!" Gregory picked up the flip-flop, and bounced it in his hands. "How did you get a lady friend past Mom?"

"I didn't," he said, snatching it back. "And she's not a friend. Yet."

"Whatever, or whoever, she is, don't let her distract you from your main reason for being in town."

Good thing his brother didn't know that Jasmine already had, Micah thought.

"I'll tell you what I just told my partners. I haven't made a final decision yet."

Gregory rubbed his hands together. "Good, that still gives me plenty of time to try and convince you."

Micah reached over and clapped his brother on his shoulder. "You do that, but no more food contests, okay? I'm a chef, not a pig, and those baked goods almost killed me!"

"Yeah, you said I owed you, what about it?" Gregory laughed.

"Forget it. Somebody else took care of your marker."

Jasmine had him under her spell, and didn't even know it. And now, Micah was the one who owed her.

He had to see her again, had to convince her to let him take her to his friend's winery. Then he could decide what to do about her, could test his ability to resist her innate seductiveness. And when he succeeded he could breathe easy again, without fearing that he might not be able to live without her.

Jasmine shoved her phone in the back pocket of her jeans. She was furious with herself for checking to see if Micah had called. She guessed he didn't like being rejected once, let alone twice.

Lucy joined her behind the bar. "I'm so glad Donnie removed that section of the counter. It's so nice not having to lift it up and down again every time we come back here."

Jasmine didn't reply and slapped a dry dishtowel over her shoulder so hard a couple of the patrons at the bar looked up. Well, she didn't take kindly to men who kissed her senseless and disappeared like the air in a worn out tire.

"He was the one who stopped kissing me first," she muttered under her breath, as she poured a beer. After Jasmine gave the drink to a customer, she stuffed his two-dollar tip in the jar.

"What did you say, honey?" Lucy asked, handing her some sliced limes and lemons. "Nothing, Lucy. I'm just wondering when I'm going to stop being a fool for men."

Her grandmother, who never married, laughed. "Women have been asking themselves that same question for years, probably beginning with Eve."

"And nobody has an answer yet?" Jasmine asked, shaking her head.

"Not for lack of trying," Lucy said, patting her on the shoulder.

"Tell me about it," she replied, rolling her eyes.

She handed a tray of dirty glasses to Donnie, and then began adding clean ones to another tray underneath the bar.

"I just can't figure out why a man shows interest in a woman one minute and dashes away the next."

"Who is the man who has you so rankled this morning?"

Jasmine bit her lip, wondering if she should tell her, and then decided that it couldn't hurt. She trusted her grandmother implicitly, and it would feel good to get some of her frustrations out.

She bent close to Lucy's ear, not wanting to take the chance that someone might hear.

"Micah Langston, and by the way, you were completely right about him."

Jasmine had decided that he was a bona fide flirt, and it was too bad she would never find out if he could be anything more to her. She didn't even know if he was still in town, but he was stuck in her fantasies, and she was stuck right along with him.

Lucy raised a brow and laughed. "Ah! The Langston men strike again. Micah, our hometown celebrity chef, is cooking up some trouble for you, eh?"

Jasmine frowned. "No, he isn't. That's the problem."

"Give him time, honey, and he'll come around."

"He doesn't even live here, Lucy," Jasmine urged with a low voice. "He was only visiting."

"And so he'll be back. This is the town in which he was born. No one who truly loves Bay Point can ever leave for good. This place can get stuck in your heart, like sand in your shoes, if you let it."

Jasmine scrunched up her nose. She hated getting sand anywhere, but especially in her shoes, which is why she wore flip-flops. One of which was now in Micah's possession, and it looked like she wasn't ever going to get it back. She didn't want it, but she did still want him.

Her heart clenched in her chest, and she couldn't deny she was hurt. All the more reason why she should concentrate on the one person she loved most in the world.

She wrapped her arms around her grandmother and gave her a big hug. “Thank you for listening, Lucy. I’m sorry if I seemed down for the past few days.”

Lucy kissed her on the cheek. “I’m always here for you.”

They parted and Jasmine glanced about the room, nearly empty of lunchtime customers. The day after she’d won the bake-off, they’d had a huge crowd. Everyone asked for her award-winning Triple Berry Crumb Crust pie, having gotten the impression that it was currently available at the restaurant. They were very disappointed to learn that it was not, and some had not come back.

Lucy was open to adding it to the menu, but Jasmine wasn’t so sure. Deep down, she feared her win at the bake-off was merely a fluke, or a stroke of good luck. She wanted to have at least one more dessert, in case that one flopped.

Jasmine took care of the final customer and handed her a copy of the receipt. When she was gone, she locked the door and hopped on a barstool.

“Another lunchtime rush is over. It’s time for me to listen to you, Gram. You’ve wanted to discuss something ever since I won the bake-off, but every time I try to find out what it is, you won’t tell me. I’m not prepping for dinner until you do.”

“You drive a hard bargain.” Lucy smiled, poured two glasses of sweet tea and handed her one. “How do you like living in Bay Point?”

She took a sip, and closed her eyes briefly, enjoying the drink's refreshing taste. "I'm getting used to it. The pace is different, but I really like being with you, and learning about everything you do."

"Running a restaurant isn't at all like those glossy brochures and fancy videos you worked on in New Orleans, is it?"

"Not at all, it's better." Jasmine couldn't believe she was saying that, but it was true. "I love the fact that we help people connect with each other, and with the community.

Lucy nodded. "Our food, hearkens back to my mother, your great-grandmother. Our Louisiana roots bridge the past with the present, and bring people together."

"Those recipes I found. Those need to be shared, too."

"I know." Lucy took one of Jasmine's hands in hers. "And I need you to share them."

Jasmine tilted her head. "Me? How?"

"I've placed a call to my lawyer. In the event of my death, ownership of the restaurant will immediately transfer to you."

Jasmine set her glass back on the bar and her blood ran as cold as the ice cubes in it. "Lucy! I can't run this restaurant. Not without you!"

Lucy patted her hand. "And you won't have to, not for a long time, God willing. But now at least you'll have some…what do men say…some skin in the game?" She laughed. "A reason to stay in Bay Point, even if things don't work out with that Langston rascal."

Jasmine enveloped her grandmother's hands together in hers. "I don't care about him, Lucy. All I care about is that you stay well and happy."

"Thank you, dear. You deserve happiness, too, perhaps more than anyone." Lucy yawned. "I think I'll go upstairs and rest for a while.

Jasmine waited until she was through the swinging doors, then she folded her arms and laid her forehead against them on the bar.

What was she going to do? No doubt she wanted to continue to help her grandmother, but to stay in Bay Point forever? Man or no man, she didn't think of it as home. Not yet, anyway. Maybe not ever.

Jasmine swam up through a dream she knew she would never remember. She rubbed the sleep out of her eyes and hopped off the barstool. Glancing over, she saw Micah tapping on the front window and waving at her.

Her breath caught in her throat, and she swallowed hard in surprise. Seeing him there was better than any dream. Before she could change her mind, she walked over and unlocked the door.

"Sleeping on the job again?" he teased, walking past her.

Holding back a smile, she closed the door with her back and leaned against it.

"You've got a lot of nerve showing your face here, Micah. I won't be like everyone else in this town and ask you where you've been. You don't call. You don't write."

"I didn't want any more hang-ups, and I don't have your email."

She stared at the exposed brick wall that held a framed collection of vintage advertisements.

"Excuses, excuses."

He approached her as if to give her a hug, but she held out her hand and pushed him into the nearest blue vinyl booth.

"Hey! I came here to apologize to you."

But she barely heard him and went on. "This is all very weird. You're kissing me, and I'm kissing you, and we're not talking and..."

He caught one of her flailing hands and pulled her onto his lap.

"What do you think you're doing?"

Micah placed a finger on her lips. "Shhh. Stop ranting and let me explain."

"The day after we met at the pier, I had to fly to Portland. There was a problem with one of the refrigeration units in my restaurant and I had to go purchase a new one."

She raised a brow. "I would think you would have someone who would do that for you."

"I do. But Sheila, my director of operations, was at my other restaurant in New York City. I was closer, so it made sense that I fly up and take care of it myself."

His explanation did not take away the sleepless nights and endless worrying. Still Jasmine was relieved that the reason for his disappearance had nothing to do with her.

"Let me make it up to you," Micah cajoled.

He tried to put his arms around her, but she sprang out of his lap. The man wasn't out of the doghouse yet.

She slid into the other side of the booth. "How?"

"My original offer is still open," he said, folding his hands.

Jasmine leaned back against the booth. "Anything else?"

"I've got a few things in mind." He grinned. "But you've got to accept the others first. Dinner, private lesson, winery."

"Seems like we'll be spending a lot of time together."

"That's the whole point isn't it? To see if we really like each other."

"To see if you'll really stick around."

"You're not going to let me off easy, are you?"

It was her turn to grin. She leaned over and poked him in his chest. "Not on your life, buddy."

He caught her finger and nuzzled his lips against it. Tingles of pleasure shot rapid-fire up her arm and across her chest. She closed her eyes, and the next thing she knew, his mouth was on hers, and she was kissing him back.

For a while, Jasmine was unaware of anything but their warm, wet tongues. They kissed deeply, with the table a barrier between their bodies, but not to their heat. She fought the urge to crawl up and over the Formica and land in his lap.

She broke away, gasping, but he caught her cheeks in his hands and kissed her again.

"Does this prove how sorry I am," he muttered. "And how much I missed you?"

Jasmine shook her head to break his kiss, afraid that Gloria or Donnie might walk in. She slipped away from the table and stood. "It's a good start, but I have things to do to get ready for the dinner rush."

He slouched back against the booth, watching her. "Rush? I heard that dinner was Lucy's weakest seating."

Something in his tone sounded accusatory, and she felt she had to protect her grandmother.

"You should know better than to listen to idle gossip." She walked over to the window and peeked outside. "That space across the street, for example. Nobody knows what's going in there. It's commercial space, so obviously there will be some kind of business."

"Any idea what kind?"

"No, but the rumors are flying. Lucy and I are hoping for a grocery store. It would be awesome to be able to walk across the street and go shopping."

He nodded, and seemed relieved. "You're right. I'm glad to hear that Lucy is doing well. I want you to know if there's anything I can ever do to help, I'm here."

Except when you're not, she thought, wanting to believe that he was being sincere, but not ready to trust him just yet.

"Thank you. I'll let my grandmother know. Now, if you'll excuse me, I've got to get back to work."

Micah got up and sauntered over. "I'm not going anywhere until you give me your decision on my offer."

She put her hands on her hips. "If I say yes, will you promise to leave me alone?"

"First, you want me. Then you don't."

She laughed at his light tone. "I guess we're both acting fickle, aren't we?"

"All the more reason we should spend time together and straighten each other out. Otherwise, we'll just drive each other crazy."

He propped his chin on one fist, and tilted his head. "Come to think of it, that might be fun."

"Might be fun?" Jasmine play-punched him in the shoulder. "Winery, yes. Dinner, no. I'll need plenty of notice so I can get someone to fill in for me here."

He gave her a peck on the cheek. "We can schedule it for a day that would work for you, just let me know."

As she locked the door behind him, she told herself that she only agreed because she wanted to show Lucy that she was learning how to cook more types of foods besides cakes and pastries. She hoped a few general lessons would also make it less daunting for her to prepare some of the more challenging family recipes.

Thinking of all the ways this date with Micah could eventually help Lucy lessened her anxiety. She knew that rushing into a relationship with him would be a mistake. She had to slow down things down to a simmer, and maybe, she could somehow forget just how good he made her feel.

Chapter 5

Micah walked down the steps, stopping every few moments to stretch one hamstring, and then the other, until he landed on the sand. One of the best things about his parents' private estate was access to their own private beach.

A perpetual renter in three states, he didn't own any residential real estate, not yet anyway. He could never decide where or what to buy, and besides, as a single guy, he didn't need the space, nor the hassle of the upkeep, preferring to stay mobile and unencumbered.

After a few more stretches to limber up, he walked down to the shore, where the sand was packed and wet.

With the wind at his back, he set off south, toward the pier. A nice easy pace, the salt in the air tickled his nose, his mood as buoyant as his steps. He dodged tumbling waves and laughed at the sandpipers, but not at himself, not anymore.

His social life had lost its monotony, courtesy of Jasmine Kennedy, and instead of wondering *what now*, he was excited about what it could be.

In a few days, he and Jasmine would be spending the day together, completely alone. He couldn't wait. Micah didn't know if she was the one, but she was the woman he wanted to be with right now. Whenever he thought about her, he smiled and couldn't stop.

Sure, he worried about the future, but that was restricted to his professional life. His two business partners, plus one hundred and fifty employees counted on him for their livelihoods. He also had a responsibility to his customers to ensure the food he served was the highest quality.

All of that burdened his mind, so when it came to his personal life, he liked to live in the moment. That way, he was always surprised.

He sighed and thought about his meeting yesterday with Liza Marbet, who had agreed to submit a design proposal. She had no issues with signing a nondisclosure agreement, which brought it now to half a dozen people in town who knew his secret and that made him very, very nervous.

In the distance, he saw his brother Marlon jogging toward him, and he picked up his pace. Then Jasmine appeared from behind and settled in, running right next to him.

Micah swore under his breath and deliberately slowed down. He wanted to watch the interaction between them, before jumping to all kinds of conclusions. Even though he already had them in bed together in his mind.

Marlon was a self-proclaimed mixologist and a player of the worst kind. He knew it, he enjoyed it, and he was never going to change. To him, women were both a creative inspiration and a physical distraction to his attempts at writing a novel.

Even their parents had given up hope that he would marry. Since they were teenagers, he and Gregory had avoided introducing their girlfriends to him, knowing he would do everything in his power to steal them away.

He frowned as he watched Jasmine and Marlon laughing as if they didn't have a care in the world. Had she even noticed him at all?

Finally, he dropped down to one knee and pretended to retie his shoe. When they were almost upon him, he stood up.

"Good morning," he said, before either could speak. "I didn't know you had such a beautiful running partner, Marlon."

Jasmine halted in her tracks. "Hello, Micah."

"Oh. Do you two know each other?" Marlon asked.

"Not really," Jasmine said quickly. "I met Micah at Lucy's. Marlon and I are training for a half marathon together."

"Is that all?" he asked, trying hard to tamp down on his jealousy.

Marlon glanced between him and Jasmine. "Yeah, what else would there be? By the way, how are the plans going?"

Micah furrowed his brow. "Plans?"

"The ones for the old—"

Micah swooped his hand through a wave, pretending to wash them. He deliberately splashed water on Marlon's shoes, so he wouldn't spill the beans about his meeting with the architect.

"Ooops, sorry."

Marlon tried to jump out of the way, but it was too late. "Micah! These shoes cost me three hundred dollars. Now they're sopping wet. I can't run in these."

Micah squinted up at the sun, hiding a smile. "I guess you better go home and change."

Marlon gave him a disgusted look, and then slipped off his shoes and socks. "Sorry, Jasmine. Same time, tomorrow?"

She nodded, and they watched him run barefoot down toward the estate.

Jasmine turned. "That was a dirty trick."

"I can do a lot of things, but I can't control nature," he shrugged. "Why didn't you tell him you knew me?"

She put her hands on her hips. "I could ask the same thing of you."

"I don't discuss my private life with my family."

"And I don't discuss my private life with strangers."

"I don't qualify as a stranger, Jasmine. Not anymore. And you know it."

She pointed a finger at him. "We haven't spent more than an hour together and you're already acting like you own me."

Micah raised his hands to his chest. "I'm sorry. It's just that my brother isn't the man for you."

"And you are?"

"Maybe, but he's definitely not. He's a player."

Jasmine struck a defiant pose. "He's a nice guy and we have great conversations."

"About what?"

"Brainstorming, mostly. He tells me his new drink ideas, and I tell him my new recipes for cakes and cookies."

"Wait a minute, do you mean to tell me that when you're running, you talk about food?"

Jasmine nodded. "What's wrong with that?"

"Most people want to avoid talking about what started them exercising in the first place."

"Unlike you and I," she said. "Marlon and I are on the same wavelength. That is, until you came along."

"I highly doubt that. There's only one thing Marlon cares about and it's not how to make the best martini."

"Why is it that every time I see you there always has to be an argument?" she said.

"I'm just trying to protect you."

She folded her arms. "Oh? I just thought you were trying to get into my pants."

He stared at her, openmouthed. Yes, he wanted her, more than anything, but he never realized he was being so transparent. His game needed a serious skill update.

Although he was afraid how he would act if he actually fell in love with her, he didn't want her to think that he wanted her just for sex.

"You mean more to me than that, Jasmine."

She didn't respond. Instead she turned and walked away toward the pier, and his heart fell.

"Where are you going?"

"I'm off my pace, and maybe I'm out of my mind."

He caught up with her and stepped in front of her. "You feel it, too, don't you?"

"Yeah. I'm tired, sore and cranky."

"That's not what I mean and you know it."

She shook her head, but there was a hint of a smile as he tilted her chin up. He resisted the urge to kiss her.

"I've got a cure for all three of those conditions. Are you still interested?"

She nodded, and he knew that the wariness he saw in her eyes was his fault. He had to redouble his efforts to show that he cared. He didn't want her to fall in love with him, but he didn't want her to hate him, either.

"Perfect. I'll see you Saturday."

As she jogged away, he knew it would take more than dinner and drinks to soothe away her caution.

Micah jogged up the stairs from the beach to the patio of his parents' estate, and was surprised to see Marlon waiting for him.

"I'm sorry. I know I almost messed things up for you back there."

"Yeah, you did," Micah replied, struggling to keep the annoyance out of his tone. Although his brother made some stupid mistakes sometimes, he knew he didn't mean to cause trouble. "In more ways than one."

"I thought it was strange that you had everyone, including your family, sign nondisclosure agreements, but now I understand why."

"Good, then I can trust you'll never let your mouth flow like an open beer tap again?"

Marlon held up his hand. "You have my word."

"Are you seeing her?"

"No! I just met her a couple of months ago."

Micah's lips edged out a wry grin. "Length of time known has never stopped you in the past."

"Geez. Give me a little credit, will you? She's gorgeous, but not my type."

"Good. Keep it that way," he said, and strolled into the house to escape further questioning.

Micah knew he had to make a decision about the restaurant soon. He wasn't exactly lying to Jasmine, but he wasn't telling the truth either. Keeping secrets would destroy any chance at a long-term relationship, if he decided he wanted one with her.

Jasmine arranged two red carnations and a sprig of baby's breath in a small milk glass vase. Yesterday, she'd visited Blooms in Paradise and negotiated a fair price for the hardy flowers and greenery, plus weekly delivery.

A couple of weeks ago, she'd found a box of vintage vases in the storeroom, and asked her grandmother if she could use them. Lucy agreed that it would be nice to have something other than salt and pepper shakers and assorted condiments on the tables.

Jasmine looked around the restaurant, smiled and decided that bringing back something from the past could really add charm. She hoped her guests would appreciate the decorative touch.

After hurrying back to the bar, she looked at the three decadent desserts laid out for the scheduled taste testing: Coconut Cake, Crème Brûlée and her award-winning Triple Berry Crumb Crust Pie. Today was important to the future of Lucy's. She had to get everything right.

She took in a shuddering breath, still reeling from her conversation with Micah a few days earlier. Although it flattered her that he seemed to be jealous of her friendship with his brother, it scared her, too. She didn't want a possessive man; she just wanted to feel like she was the most important person in his life, while not having to give up her own.

Was that why she hadn't bothered to tell Micah that she was training for a marathon with his brother? When Lucy made the comment that the Langston men were flirts, she thought it was strange because Marlon, whom she'd met first, had never acted that way with her.

Marlon seemed lonely and distracted, but appeared to be a good guy. From the very beginning, Jasmine had the sense that he wasn't attracted to her at all, which was a relief. She could concentrate on preparing for the half marathon and not have to worry about him hitting on her.

The man was an exercise partner, and nothing more, yet Micah acted like she was sleeping with him. It was frustrating, but it made her think that he had feelings for her, beyond attraction, that maybe he didn't understand.

She did, too, and she would explore those feelings at the winery date, away from the pressures of the restaurant that would someday be her own.

Gloria emerged from the kitchen, carrying three place settings on a large tray.

"Which table are you going to use?"

"Let's set up in a booth. Maisie prefers the one farthest from the door."

The two women got to work. The white bone china that had once belonged to her great-grandmother might be plain, but it would put all the focus on her desserts. The heavy embossed silverware had been recently polished. Three blue chintz cloth napkins finished the French country look.

After they were done, Jasmine thanked Gloria, who went back into the kitchen to continue making dinner.

Lucy walked into the dining area. "Everything looks beautiful. The bud vases are a nice touch."

Jasmine hugged her. "Thanks for letting me do the taste testing."

"It's a good idea, especially inviting Maisie. That woman has no shortage of opinions. If she likes everything, everyone in town will know it."

"Free advertising!" Then Jasmine frowned. "But if she doesn't, I might as well hang up my apron."

"I'm sure she will," Lucy reassured her, as someone knocked at the door. "Maisie loves her sweets almost as much as she loves Bay Point."

Jasmine plastered a nervous smile on her face, walked over and opened the door. "Welcome, ladies!"

Lucy greeted Maisie with a warm hug. "It's been a while!"

Maisie stepped inside and laughed. "I was here for

breakfast yesterday morning. Why I consider this place an extension of my own kitchen!"

"I'm not surprised," Jasmine said. "You live so close. The restaurant is practically a hop, skip and a jump away."

"Rather, a hobble and a limp when my hip is bad," Maisie chuckled. "But Lucy's food is always worth the pain."

She proceeded to introduce the two other women who had entered the restaurant after her. Jasmine didn't recognize either of them. "This is Liza Marbet, a local architect, and Randi Tilly, an aspiring actress who is a guest at the B&B for a couple of nights."

"Welcome to you both," Jasmine said, as she led everyone to the booth.

Once the ladies were settled in their seats, Donnie served their choice of either coffee or tea.

Jasmine handed them three small cards, each with the name of the dessert notated on it, and a pencil.

"Thank you again for coming today. Here are the three desserts you will taste this afternoon. On the back of the card, please rate each from one to ten, with ten being the best."

Donnie brought over a tray of three servings of her triple berry pie and distributed them.

"Ladies, you are in for a treat," Maisie said, digging in. "I snuck a tiny sliver at the bake-off before it went to the judges, and I thought I'd died and gone to heaven a second time."

"When was the first time?" Randi asked.

Maisie swallowed and winked. "When Micah Langston walked into the judges' room. That man looks as tasty as he is talented."

"Dessert before dinner. I can't think of anything more decadent," Liza said.

"I can," Randi giggled, holding up a picture of Micah on her cell phone.

Liza's lips twitched, and she appeared to be holding back a smile. "Whoa! I'm sorry I missed the event. He's gorgeous."

He certainly is, Jasmine thought, and she was glad that Micah didn't hang around the restaurant on a regular basis. They weren't a couple yet, and only they knew the state of their relationship. If it failed to take off, no one but them would know it.

Plates were cleared, fresh silver was handed out and three-layer coconut cake slices were placed before each woman.

"Every time I take a bite of coconut I feel like I'm back on the Islands," Randi said. "This is so delicious."

"Thank you," Jasmine beamed. "Where are you from originally?"

"Jamaica," Randi replied. "I'll be leaving in a few days to visit my sister in Los Angeles."

"How exciting!" Liza said. "How did you learn about Bay Point?"

"My agent's great-aunt was an actress back in the late fifties. She used to come here on the weekends."

When they were finished eating the cake, the women scribbled their remarks on the back of the menu. After a second round of beverages, the final dessert, Crème Brûlée, was given. It, too, was well received.

"Are there other bakeries in town?" Randi asked.

"Ruby's Tasty Pastries," Jasmine responded. "But she makes her own breads and other small baked goods, like cookies, doughnuts and croissants. She doesn't really do desserts."

Liza took a sip of her tea. "That's good to hear, but I'm afraid there will continue to be competition for wallets in this town."

Maisie's ears perked up. "Anything you care to share?"

"I can't disclose anything, but I've been contacted by several individuals looking to open up new businesses downtown who want my design ideas."

"They probably heard about the wonderful work you did on your husband's clinic," Maisie replied.

Liza smiled. "I'm just glad to have some potential clients. I want to have my architecture firm well established before Anthony and I start a family."

Randi chimed in. "I'm glad I don't own a business, but competition keeps everyone on their toes and provides consumers with a choice."

Jasmine inwardly agreed, although she knew that her grandmother felt differently. For years, Lucy's Bar and Grille had been the only dining option in Bay Point. The town was growing, times were changing and Lucy needed to realize that she and the restaurant had to change with them.

"Anyone know what's going into the space across the street?" Jasmine asked, as she helped Donnie clear the dishes. "I went over there one night and thought I saw a light moving around inside."

Everyone shrugged. "Surprisingly, I haven't heard anything," Maisie said. "But I'll let you know if I do."

Jasmine nodded, and handed out some gift certificates for the restaurant as thank-you gifts.

"You should do this more often, Jasmine," Maisie said. "I think a lot of people would be tickled to go to a dessert-before-dinner event like this."

"Yeah, you could couple it with a wine tasting. That would be really fun," Liza suggested.

"That's not such a bad idea. I'm actually going to a winery this weekend and can ask about appropriate pairings for our current menu and these treats, too."

After everyone left, Jasmine sank into a booth and read the comments. Overall, the event had been a success.

Her next challenge was to keep her time with Micah on Saturday in the "it's only a date" lane. It was going to be very difficult to do so after all the nights of dreaming about him, the distracted days at work and those in-between times when he crept into her mind for no reason at all.

But the longing in her heart had to be ignored. The winery trip was for business purposes only.

Chapter 6

"Hot little car," Jasmine told Micah, as she stepped into the red convertible. It sat so low to the ground she was glad she'd done her squats that morning.

His gaze was equally hot on her as she arranged her tote bag and purse at her feet, and slipped off her sandals. He'd suggested that she dress casually, so she wore faded denim shorts and a white eyelet tank top.

"You're lucky I didn't pick you up in a rusted-out, station wagon."

"Why the ire, Micah?" she asked, politely, though she could guess the reason.

He slid his sunglasses to the top of his head. "Not ire, irritation. Why couldn't I pick you up at Lucy's?"

Lucy thought she was spending the day at the beach. That's why she asked him to meet her at the parking lot. She couldn't risk her grandmother or worse, Maisie, finding out that she was going anywhere with him.

It wasn't that she cared about what they might say. She was more worried about what they might think about her, should their relationship not work out.

Jasmine looked over at him and smiled. "What difference does it make? I'm here."

His eyes turned amused before he covered them up again with his sunglasses. "In that case, let's roll."

She waited until they were on the Pacific Coast Highway to speak again. "So, where are we headed?"

"A little winery near Mendocino." He gave her an appreciative glance. "What you're wearing is perfect. This is not one of those uppity places."

She smiled at him, loving that despite being rich and famous, he was so down-to-earth. "Good, because I don't do uppity anything."

Since agreeing to the day trip, Jasmine had tried everything she could think of to tamp down her initial enthusiasm, so that she wouldn't get her hopes up. She didn't go out and buy a new outfit, agonize over her hair or fuss with her makeup.

She even searched gossip sites for any juicy tidbits about Micah that might make her want to call the whole date off.

She learned that he'd never been married or had children. There were a few mentions of the women he'd dated in the past, but nothing earth-shattering. Even she was surprised that she didn't feel threatened by the looks or achievements of his former flames, which made it even odder that Micah appeared to be jealous of her acquaintance with his younger brother.

She wriggled her pink-painted toes, and admired her nails of the same color. A mani-pedi and a facial were her only expenses, and they were always well worth it.

Jasmine settled her back more comfortably against the bucket seat and turned her gaze toward Micah. She should be working with Lucy at the restaurant rather than sitting in this beautiful car next to a gorgeous man. But her grandmother had been so sweet, and had insisted that she needed a break, and not just for fifteen minutes. She felt a tinge of guilt for not being honest about her plans for the day.

"What's that look for?" Micah said, a smile on his face.

She debated telling him about her new focus for the date, tasting wines for the restaurant, but decided to keep it to herself. He looked so happy to be with her that she didn't want to spoil his mood.

"It's a thank-you," she replied, grinning back. "I really needed this."

Micah put his hand on her knee. She liked his gentle squeeze, the possessive warmth that said "you're mine."

"I'd rather have a kiss."

She felt a little thrill in her loins at his words. His wicked tone made her admit to herself how exciting it was to be with him. This man had the power to turn her on just by opening his mouth.

"And I'd rather get to the winery in one piece," she admonished with a laugh. He removed his hand and looked so forlorn that moments later, she leaned over and nuzzled the underside of his jaw with her mouth.

He groaned and his hands gripped the steering wheel even tighter as she moved her lips toward his earlobe.

"We won't get anywhere but the side of the road, if you keep that up."

She stopped abruptly, though she wanted to keep teasing him, wanted to put her hand on his thigh and slowly inch north. It was enough to know that she could rile him up, too.

Jasmine leaned her head back against the headrest as Micah turned up the tunes. The wind whipped through her hair, tempering the heat of the morning sun, but not the smile on her lips. Her grin widened, cliff to guardrail, and she started laughing, hands up in the air as the convertible hugged the curves of the Pacific Coast Highway.

This woman could change everything, Micah thought as he pulled off the exit and headed east.

He reached over to wake her, but decided to let her sleep. She looked so peaceful and it wouldn't be long before they reached their destination.

Besides, he liked being able to sneak glances at her petite figure. The black leather seat fit her like a glove, and he suspected he would, too. God knows he wanted to try, to see how they fit together.

He hardened instantly at the thought of making love to her, but only if she wanted it, though he wasn't really worried. It was only a matter of time before everything he dreamed about would become a reality.

They couldn't tease and flirt forever. It was like sweating in the hot sun, with the waves licking at your feet. Sooner or later, you had to wade in, cool off, and then emerge, only to heat up again.

And he was sizzling for Jasmine Kennedy. From the moment he saw her, he wanted her for his own. Maybe not for life, but he couldn't rule that out either. Because if it was as good as he thought it was going to be, he would lay claim to her—heart, body and soul—and never let her go.

At a red light, he reached out and ran his finger down the side of her long, slender neck. She stirred a little, and he watched her breasts move with her deep breath. She didn't awaken, just snuggled back against the seat even more.

He frowned at her obvious exhaustion, and felt bad that she had to work so hard. But he liked the fact that she was in the same business as he, and he knew he could teach her a lot, if she'd let him. He'd learned much over the past ten years that could make her and Lucy's lives easier.

But teaching her about the restaurant business would make it even harder to keep his plans a secret. Soon, they could be competing for customers. And from his experience, Lucy and Jasmine would be no match against Society Red.

He had more money, more brand recognition and quite frankly, the power to shut them down forever. He'd done it before and he could do it again. For his partners, for his reputation. It wasn't personal. It was business. Though the people his ambition affected never believed him. They just thought he was a selfish prick.

Whatever he ultimately decided to do in Bay Point, he'd have to leave his heart out of it once again. The more time he spent with Jasmine, the harder that would be to do.

Thirty minutes later, he turned onto a gravel driveway and stopped at the security gate. He punched in a code that had been given to him and the gates swung open.

"Wake up, sleepyhead," he said, gently nudging her arm with his elbow. "We're here."

"Where are we?" Her eyes blinked open. "This is the winery?"

He shot her a grin. "You won't find this place in the yellow pages. It's completely private."

"What's the name of it?" she asked.

"Doesn't have one. It's not open to the public, only by invitation."

Jasmine flipped down the mirror and gasped. "My hair is a mess after that long drive."

"I'll just mess it up even more, later."

"You better not," she warned, giggling as she ran her fingers through it. "Or you're going to owe me a hair appointment."

"I'm prepared to help pamper more than your hair, little lady."

Her lips rounded in surprise, and he was ready to go into more detail, but he saw the owner directing him to park under a grove of orange trees.

Micah pulled the car up, braked and pressed a button to close the convertible top. After securing it, he got out of the car and greeted his friend.

"It's good to see you, Zack. Thanks for having us out today."

Jasmine got out and rounded the car, tote bag and purse in one hand.

He draped his arm around her shoulder. "I'd like you to meet my best friend and the owner of the winery, Zack Smaden."

"Why didn't you tell me I'd be meeting your future wife?"

Micah had to give Jasmine credit, at least her jaw didn't drop all the way to the ground, he thought with a slow grin. Zack had a way of shocking people, whether with his food, his wine or his words. They'd been friends since culinary school, and he didn't mind his unpredictable nature.

"It's a pleasure to meet you, Zack, but we're just friends," Jasmine said, with a cool smile.

"Good, then you're still available?" he asked, giving Micah a wink.

"Nope, sorry. Jasmine is absolutely taken." He folded her into his arms, and her sharp intake of breath gave him a little jolt in the pit of his stomach. "By me."

She nudged him sharply in the ribs. "Not so fast, buddy."

"Ow!" he grunted, almost doubling over, but he stopped when he saw that she was smiling.

"We have to eat first," she said, hands curved around her hips. "I'm starved."

Both men openly stared at her, and Micah knew what

was going through both of their minds had nothing to do with food.

Zack put his hands up to his chest and took two steps back. "I'm not getting in the middle of this."

Micah started to laugh. Deep, resounding belly laughs of relief as Jasmine joined in.

"Then help me, man! Get me some wine and cheese, quick!"

"Follow me." Zack laughed. "I'll give you a quick tour first and then you are free to roam, and eat and drink."

After a brief tour of the beautiful vineyards and a small, underground cave that held his wines, Zack led them to a small, Craftsman-style bungalow.

"This is my guest home for you to use during your stay today. Please make yourself comfortable."

Zack turned to Micah. "I have everything you requested. You are free to use either the indoor or outdoor kitchen." He held up his phone. "Just text me if you need anything at all."

When he left, Micah somehow managed to keep a straight face, despite the fact that he was so excited about the day ahead he could burst.

Jasmine followed him in to the kitchen and folded her arms. "What are you up to?"

"Up to?" Micah opened the refrigerator and glanced over his shoulder.

Every time he looked at Jasmine, she seemed to morph into something more beautiful than before. His eyes were fine, twenty-twenty vision. It wasn't the wine, as he hadn't had any yet. It wasn't that he felt inwardly pressured to compliment her.

She just plain wowed him.

"Don't play innocent with me," she warned with a shake of a finger.

He shut the refrigerator and took the plastic wrap off a tray of French artisanal cheeses. He picked one up with a toothpick and walked over to her.

"Shhh." He kissed her more quickly than he wanted to, then fed her a piece of cheese.

"Hmm, it's so creamy. What is this?" she asked, her mouth full.

"Cantalet, from Auvergne in south-central France, made with cow's milk. It will pair very nicely with Zack's Cabernet."

"Which you still haven't opened yet," she said, snagging another piece of cheese from the tray.

He grabbed the corkscrew Zack had left him, and got to work. "By the way, I'm not up to anything," he said, after pouring them two generous glasses.

He clinked his gently to hers. "Other than making you happy, for today at least."

"Just today?" she asked, taking a slow sip.

He did the same, and raised his glass. "Today is all we've got, and I intend to take full advantage of it."

"So where do we start, Micah?"

"Right here, or rather outside." He picked up the bottle of wine and motioned her to follow him. "It's too nice to cook inside today. Will you help me take everything to the kitchen out there?"

"No problem."

He slid open the patio door and they placed their wine glasses on the bistro table.

"I hope you aren't a picky eater."

"Only when I'm cooking," she said, laughing. "What's on the menu?"

"You know I love barbecue, so I've got to show you how to move around a grill."

They went back into the house. Micah stood in front of the refrigerator and handed her the ingredients for the food he planned to prepare. Jasmine placed them in a two-handled basket so that she could carry everything in one trip.

"How does Chipotle Orange Chicken, and Portobello Mushrooms Stuffed with Spinach and Artichoke sound?"

Jasmine smiled. "Yummy! I'm ready to learn."

Once they got everything outside, Micah started the grill, while she washed the vegetables. He showed her how to julienne the red peppers, and how to properly debone a chicken.

"So tell me about Zack. Where did you meet?"

Micah laid each piece of chicken carefully on the grill. "Culinary school in Hyde Park. He was a very successful executive chef at several Michelin-rated restaurants in Los Angeles, and then decided to become a vintner. As he said on the tour, tastings are private and by appointment alone."

"Did he say why he decided to change careers?"

"No, he never said, and I didn't ask."

He refreshed their glasses, finishing off the first bottle. "Besides, does anybody really need a reason for doing something that they love?"

They both sat down, and Jasmine propped her feet on his lap. "I'm surprised he didn't make us squish the grapes with our toes."

He cupped her heels in his hands and began to massage them. "Do you really want to ruin that pretty pedicure?"

"You would just have to paint them again," she smiled, demurely, as she fought not to squirm with pleasure in her seat.

Micah raised a brow, and he massaged his way to her toes, and then slowly back to her ankles. "Feel good?"

She took a sip of wine and placed the glass back on the small table next to her.

"Oh yes, definitely. I could get used to this."

He pulled her onto his lap, fully aware that he was already hard for her. He wanted her to know it, too.

"So could I, Jasmine."

Micah nuzzled her neck for a long time, petting her with his nose, swabbing her ear with his tongue, loving the way her soft moans vibrated against his lips.

He cupped her cheek with his hand and stroked it gently with his fingers. Her skin felt silky smooth.

"What are you thinking right now?" he asked, gazing into her eyes.

She wriggled her ass, getting more comfortable in his lap. Her soft roundness seemed to do a slow melt into him and Micah fought the urge to grab on to it.

"That I don't want to think about anything."

Micah touched his forehead to hers. "I can certainly take care of that for you."

He kissed her tenderly at first, from one corner of her mouth to the other. With one hand clasped at the back of her neck, he made every millimeter of her wet and luscious lips pop with pleasure.

He melded his lips to hers, teasing them open with his tongue. She welcomed him with a low moan of his name. Their tongues, tasting of wine, darted in and out of their mouths, in a sort of cat-and-mouse game, of which both were the winners.

Micah paused and gazed into her eyes before delving his tongue into the soft indent of skin at the base of her neck. She threw her head back and grabbed his head with her hands as he planted kisses along the ridge of her collarbone.

Jasmine played with the tiny curls at the back of his head, her fingers trying to grab purchase where there was none, as she squirmed and twisted in his lap.

Without lifting his lips from her skin, he twisted, too, trying to get comfortable, but his growing manhood made that impossible. She seemed to realize it, or maybe she just wanted to feel him, because the next thing he knew, she was straddling him.

Though they were both still clothed, he could feel her hot sex on him, and he moved his hips to get as close as he could. She moaned against his neck, and then kissed him from collarbone to ear, her lips like fire on his skin.

Micah massaged his hands up and down her back in slow motion as Jasmine swiveled her pelvis against him. He joined her, matching her movements, until they were both breathless.

Jasmine abruptly stopped moving and leaned her forehead against his shoulder, but still maintained the pressure of her sex against his rock-hard penis. She was panting slightly, and he knew that her body had almost gone over the edge from their grinding together, so she was holding back.

He gathered her into his arms and kissed her gently to calm her down. He was pleased that she wanted to wait and take things slowly. With her help, he slipped her tank over her head, until he was face-to-face with the sheerest lace bra he'd ever seen. It seemed as fragile as the sensual moment between them, so much so that he was almost afraid to touch her.

But then his desire for her took over. His mouth began to water, and he began to trace the swell of her cleavage with the tip of one finger. She wasn't overly huge, nor small either, but she was perfect for him and he started to lean in.

Before his mouth landed, he looked up into her face. He had to be sure before proceeding further. Her eyes were bright with desire for him, and he felt his heart quicken when she took his hand and laid it on her breast to encourage him to go on. He could have kissed her for that, and he would, but right now he had to taste her.

"Jasmine, I've dreamed about you."

He let his eyes cast hungrily over her sweet-looking flesh, to her dark nipple and even darker areola pooled around it, both so thinly veiled beneath the sheer fabric. He could have sworn her nipples hardened just from his gaze.

With a quick swallow, he unclasped her bra from behind, releasing her breasts. He was delighted to find them more beautiful than he'd imagined, her nipples like flower buds ready to burst.

And so was he.

Naked from the waist up was about all he could take at the moment, she was so sexy, so wanton. She was his true temptation.

"Lord, woman. I don't know where to start. You've got me perplexed."

And hard as a rock, he thought, as she began to grind against him again.

Micah gulped as she brought his head to her chest, her hips moving, her tone low and wicked. She cupped her breasts in the palms of her hands.

"Tell me which one tastes better, Chef."

He leaned his head forward and drew one tight nipple, slowly into his mouth. She lifted her chin and moaned, and he released her. The sight of her wet tit, and knowing he'd made it that way, made her moan for him, and made him immediately latch on again.

Jasmine arched her back a bit more, pressed her flat, tight abdomen against his shirt, as he massaged one breast, while suckling the other. She continued to cup her flesh in her hands, as if she wasn't willing to let him have her completely. He inhaled her scent, warm vanilla, and the taste of her in his mouth was unforgettably sweet.

Closing his eyes, he traced one nipple with his

tongue, his own excitement growing at the tight beading of her areola. Low moans rolled from her lips in approval, and as he continued the tender movements, she began to pant lightly. He kept extending the area of his moist caresses, laving outward across her soft skin until she finally dropped her hands, eyes closed, her head swaying from side to side.

He took over and raised her breasts with his own hands, gently licking the underside of each one. She grabbed his head, and her breath came in spurts, and he realized he'd discovered a very sensitive spot.

"M-Micah," she moaned, as he began to trail kisses down the center of her stomach, supporting the small of her back with his hands. "What about the food? We don't want it to burn."

Just above her navel, he swore, his balls about to burst. "I almost forgot."

He helped her to her feet, and then slipped her bra back over her arms and clasped it. "I'm only putting this on because you are a total distraction.

"Am I?"

She turned around, breathless. He pulled her to him tightly, wishing he didn't have to let her go.

He kissed the side of her neck, near her ear. His mouth salivated with need, thirsty to taste more of her.

"You know you are. Let's continue this after lunch," he murmured. "We're not even halfway done."

He watched, regretfully, as she slipped back into her tank top. But when she kissed him and moved against him again, he knew that she agreed.

Chapter 7

Jasmine propped her elbows on the granite countertop and watched Micah do his magic, still reeling from his kisses, her loins and breasts heavy with desire. Her head felt woozy, like she'd just woken up from a deep sleep, but her mind was clear. Micah Langston was a powerhouse of a man who knew how to please a woman. She could barely wait to go to bed with him.

But she would wait because judging by the delicious smells emanating from the grill she was in for a culinary treat.

They chatted while he made a black bean salad with melon and cilantro. Thunder rumbled low in the distance and they both looked up. Bay Point and much of Northern California had suffered from a serious drought for the last several years, so rain was always welcome.

"I'm glad we're under cover," Jasmine said, crossing her legs.

He picked up a pair of tongs and flipped the chicken pieces. "We're together, that's all that matters."

At his words, her thoughts turned to her ex-boss. Though she was attracted to him, she never let him know it. Nor did she ever do anything to deserve his unwanted sexual advances. The experience had left her cautious of herself and others. She'd questioned her intentions and those of every man who'd wanted to date her.

"Why are you being so good to me?"

Micah turned and raised a brow. "Do I need a reason?"

"No, but I'd still like to know."

After closing the cover of the barbecue, he washed and dried his hands.

"Listen to me. I don't want to hang a plaque on this moment. Or put it into a box and wrap it with a bow."

He braced his palms on the counter and continued. "It's like food, right? The first time you taste something new. That burst of unbelievable flavor on your tongue. The satisfaction that you were blessed enough to even sit at the table. That's how I feel when I'm with you."

Micah covered her hands with his, then her lips with kisses, and things began to heat up between them again. She was almost glad the counter separated them because it wouldn't take long before she'd be crawling over it and into his arms.

He broke the kiss, and when she opened her eyes, he was smiling into them.

"Do you associate everything with food?" she asked, smiling back.

"Not everything, but I will say this," he whispered, making the moment even more intimate. "Your lips taste amazing."

Jasmine laughed and pulled away. "Then we better stop right now before I make you even hungrier."

Micah growled in good spirit. "Help me set the table, will you?"

She found bamboo placemats, along with water glasses, plates and silverware, in the cupboard. After arranging everything on the bistro table, she opened up another bottle of wine and got two fresh wine glasses.

"Everything smells delicious, Micah."

He walked over and set a basket of bread down. "Now close your eyes while I plate everything."

She did as he asked, hiding a smile behind her hand at the seriousness of his tone.

"Bon appétit," he announced. "That's French for *dig in*."

"I know what it means," she said, opening her eyes. "I'm from New Orleans, remember?"

Jasmine inhaled the wonderful aromas in front of her. She picked up her fork and started to eat. The chicken was tender, with just enough spice. The vegetables had the perfect amount of crunch.

"Everything is so good," Jasmine said.

"Thanks! Zack made the vinaigrette that's on the salad."

"It's wonderful. He should bottle and sell it."

"I'll tell him you said so," Micah said. "When we got

here, I could tell that he liked you. So much so, I was afraid he was going to snag you away from me. He's done it before. Zack can be quite the charmer when he wants to be."

She took a sip of water. "Care to talk about it?"

"There's nothing to talk about. I didn't fight it because I didn't care about the girl."

"But you care about me?"

"Yes, I'm surprised you can't tell."

"I guess I'm just feeling overwhelmed. Everything is happening so quickly."

"Not really. You and I have been busy." He put down his wine glass and reached for her hand. "I'm willing to go at your pace. I have all the time in the world."

It started to rain, and she sat back in her chair, suddenly feeling morose and burdened. She thought of Lucy, and how she'd put her whole life into the restaurant, and wondered why she never married. She wasn't sure if she wanted to suffer the same fate.

She wanted a man. She needed a man. Someone as good and as kind as Micah, not to mention sexually stimulating.

"No you don't. None of us have enough time."

"That's true, but distractions can make us appreciate the time we have together, can't they?"

Jasmine nodded, hoping she didn't appear ungrateful. "I'm just worried that if things continue to go well between us, I won't have time for a relationship, and nor will you."

"I understand, but you told me your background is

in marketing. It's not like you're going to continue to work for Lucy for your entire life."

"Maybe I will," she said. "Lucy is going to retire soon and she wants me to take over the restaurant. I tend bar, but she wants me to learn all aspects of the business.

"Is she in good health?"

"Yes, though she is more tired than usual and can't stand on her feet as long as she used to. I think she wants to transfer ownership as soon as possible, just to be on the safe side."

The look on his face was as skeptical as she felt.

"Do you want to own and run her restaurant?"

"I'm not sure. Some days I think I do, others I don't."

"Owning any business isn't like working a nine-to-five."

"Yes," she replied sadly. "I'm learning that very quickly. Although, I enjoy meeting and talking with all the customers." She thought of a few she didn't like. "Well, most of them."

"How is business? I remember when I was a kid, it was nearly always packed." He laughed. "Lucy's had the best food."

"It still does," she asserted proudly. "We're doing okay, but we're convinced that the new gourmet burger place is one of the reasons why our dinner rush is down so dramatically. Or it could be one of the other new places."

He stared at her, and she felt her eyes begin to moisten under his gaze. It was too soon to let him know how deeply concerned she was about her grandmother and the restaurant. This was her problem to solve. Then why couldn't she stop talking about it with him?

"Lucy is worried sick. Sometimes I think her tiredness is not due to old age, but depression. I know the mayor is looking to bring even more restaurants to Bay Point, but hopefully not too many more."

"He's only trying to do what's best for the town."

Jasmine threw her napkin down on the table, her morose mood replaced with anger. She was surprised that Micah was immediately defending his brother. Didn't Micah see what was happening to her grandmother and to their town?

"Maybe the mayor should think more about what his policies are doing to the people who already live in Bay Point, as opposed to spending all his time and our tax dollars cultivating the tourist trade!"

Micah wiped his mouth and put his own napkin on the table. He held his hands up in defense.

"I'm only the man's brother. So let's not talk about him, or worse, politics. Why don't we take a walk instead?"

Jasmine tore her eyes away from him and glanced outside. "But it's raining!"

Micah shrugged and extended his hand toward her as he got out of his seat. "Minor drizzle."

She stared at him like he was crazy and opened her mouth to protest, but he shut it with a quick kiss.

"I just want to walk with you. Please?"

She looked into his eyes, nodded and clasped her hand in his.

Emerging from the patio, they both took a deep

breath, inhaling the clean, fresh air. The drizzle was light, but steady, and it felt good on her skin. Her flat-ironed hair, she knew, would curl up, soaking in the moisture. But at the moment, she didn't care.

Both barefoot, they set out toward the vineyards that held rows upon rows of plump grapes, ready to be harvested. Rolling verdant hills dotted with farmhouses and other wineries spread out to the east, the north and the south as far as she could see.

Without warning, Jasmine broke away running, laughing as Micah chased her. She ran through one row, down another, almost losing her footing several times on the wet grass.

"You can't catch me," she shouted.

"Oh I can," he insisted. "I just don't want to yet."

Looking back, she saw him lumbering behind, grinning, and she knew he was being slow on purpose, so he could watch her ass.

At the end of one row, she stopped and bent at her waist. She grabbed on to her ankles and shouted to him from between her legs.

"Come on, slow poke!" she yelled, sticking her tongue out at him, before straightening and continuing on.

Jasmine kept on running up and down the rows, and soon she didn't hear him anymore. She came to the end of the vineyard where there was a line of ancient oak trees with huge trunks, which she assumed marked the border between Zack's property and another.

Breathing heavily, Jasmine leaned against a tree, soaked to the skin, feet muddy. She started to shiver.

"Micah?"

"Boo!"

She nearly jumped to the first bough of the tree.

"You scared me half to death!"

He drew her into his arms. But peeved at him, she resisted.

Thwack! Thwack!

Her ears adjusted to the thick, sharp sound and she realized she was slapping his bare chest. She stopped immediately.

"What happened to your shirt?"

"I took a short cut and it ripped."

She planted a kiss on his hard, wet skin, on the places where she'd struck him.

"I'm sorry. I was just so startled by you jumping out from behind that tree."

His steel-like muscles flexed under her caresses, and the more she kissed him, the more she became aroused.

"I deserved it," he said, a devilish grin crossing his face. "And I kind of liked it."

She stopped and stared at him. "So did I."

This was the first time she was seeing him bare-chested and she wanted to admire him. She let her eyes roam freely across his wet skin, his ridged, muscular abdomen.

Jasmine raised her arms above her head and stretched slowly. Micah's eyes widened and she looked down and realized that her own shirt was nearly transparent.

"I like that, too," he said, his eyes dark with desire.

She blushed and crossed her arms over her breasts, suddenly embarrassed.

Micah took a step forward. "Let me see you." He uncrossed her arms, and they dropped to her side.

"Jasmine, you're beautiful."

She drew a hand through her wet hair, which had reversed back to its natural curl. "I must look a mess."

Micah caught her hand and brought it to his lips. Extending her fingers, he planted a kiss on each tip.

"No, you're perfect," he said. Extending her curled fingers gently, he planted another kiss on each one—pinky to thumb. "And I want to show you how perfect we can be together."

A little moan escaped her lips as he sucked on the tip of her thumb, and she felt her loins moistening in response.

"Right now? Right here?"

He nodded, his eyes never leaving hers. "Baby, I thought you'd never ask."

Jasmine hitched in a breath as he brought his body close. Now she could feel how hard he was for her, and as his tongue slipped into her mouth, she wrapped her arms around his neck and her legs around his waist.

He hoisted her up closer against him, licking the moisture from her neck before returning to her mouth.

Their kisses deepened. She rubbed her sex against his wet abdomen and lower still. His bulge grew larger, hotter, torturing him, torturing them. He broke the kiss and moaned against her hair, as she continued to grind against him.

"May I undress you?"

She stood and nodded dreamily, not caring that her clothes were plastered to her body. She couldn't help giggling as he struggled to remove them.

"You're not making this any easier on me, are you?"

"Don't worry," she cooed, not lifting one finger to help him, as he slid her underwear down her legs. "I'm worth the effort."

When she was completely nude, he stood back and whistled. "You aren't kidding!"

She ran her hands slowly up her body and caressed her breasts, teasing him. "Now it's your turn."

It seemed like mere seconds after she'd opened her mouth that he removed his clothes. And when they were off, she had no words. She could only stare at his long, hard length jutting out into the air, and the two dark sacs hanging behind it.

He, too, was perfect.

Kneeling, he flicked his tongue into her belly button, causing her to collapse to the ground. Her knees sank into wet grass. She giggled and squirmed as he kissed up, up, up to her chin, before landing on her mouth.

Holding her left nipple between his thumb and his forefinger, he squeezed gently and took her breath away when he replaced his touch with his tongue. He guided her onto her back as his lips sucked on one tit and then the other. Her arms moved in a languorous display across the wet grass, and she arched forward wanting more.

Micah placed his hand between her legs and her hips started to buck when he tapped lightly on that one spot that if they were behind closed doors, would make her scream.

She clenched her teeth and didn't make a sound, as she grabbed his hand and held it still against her. He began to pleasure her with his fingers, stroking and stroking, increasing the pressure and intensity of his touch.

Jasmine tilted her head to the side and watched him. The sight was almost too much for her to bear. Still, she found herself spreading her legs even wider, when he clutched one breast in his hand and latched on to her nipple again.

He licked and stroked, again and again. Her hands massaged through his hair as he nuzzled and groaned against her, making her hot and wet and sticky with lust.

"Micah, now," she whispered weakly. She tried to prop herself up on her elbows, but fell back, as the waves of pleasure he was coaxing started to build in earnest.

"Micah, please!" Jasmine begged, pulling his head away from her breast as her hips started to buck uncontrollably.

He reached back for his jeans and pulled out a condom. Her loins hurt just by watching him slowly roll it over and down his long, thick penis. He was teasing her, and taking his time doing it, too.

He moved into place between her legs and bent over her, kissing the side of her neck. "You want this?"

"Yes, damn you!" she cried, clutching his round butt with her hands.

Without another word, Micah entered her.

"Oh!" she cried out.

Her legs locked him into place and that's when he started to move. Fast and quick, like a hummingbird drawing nectar, departing then darting inside again for more. His penis felt longer and thicker every time he entered her, and she never wanted him to stop.

It started to drizzle again and his knees dug deeper into the muddy ground. He slipped down against her and she held on to his shoulders as he raised his body above hers. Not missing a beat, stroke for continuous stroke, he plunged into her again and again, his brow furrowed in deep concentration.

His gaze was so intense that he seemed to be searching for something beyond her.

Something within himself.

She understood. She was searching, too.

"Micah," she whispered, in awe of him, of how he was making her body feel.

As she closed her eyes, she felt her heart open to accept him, now or forever. Whatever the future held in store, she was ready.

Micah penetrated her again, slower and deeper than before. She lifted her buttocks off the wet grass, enjoying the hardness of his flesh as he slowly slid out again. He seemed to sense that she wanted more, and thrust again, then even deeper still. His furrowed brow became a painful grimace. He immediately stopped moving and groaned aloud.

With a loud gasp, she arched up to meet him. Their

kisses were frantic as her sensitive nipples, abraded by his tongue, smashed against his slick chest. As they rode each other to the point of sharp, yet exquisite pleasure, the clouds opened up, sending down cold shards of rain.

"We're soaked. So are our clothes."

Micah rolled onto his back, panting, satisfied, and slightly scared. The wet grass felt cool and refreshing. He'd never expected that being with Jasmine would leave him so spent yet ready for more.

She propped herself up on one elbow and gave him a slow, sweet kiss he wished could last forever. But he was cold and wet, and starting to shrivel.

"How do you propose we get inside?"

He turned and cupped one of her buttocks with his left hand. "How about I just hoist you up over my shoulder and carry you back?" he asked, only half kidding.

"Not on your life, Tarzan." She rolled her eyes and lightly slapped his buttocks in return. "Why don't we walk back as fast as we can instead? I'm freezing!"

He nodded, and they got up and picked up their sopping clothes.

With his arm around Jasmine, they made their way back to the guesthouse, Micah's heart and body felt raw and prickly. He'd made love to her in the open, on the grass and in the rain. Her sensuality was his sin, and he wanted nothing more than to continue to pleasure the woman beside him.

"I know it's a little late to ask, but I hope nobody around here has a camera," Jasmine wondered.

He saw that she was shivering even more than he

was, and he wrapped his arm around her shoulder, and pulled her close.

"Don't worry, we're miles from the next farm, and before you even ask, Zack is a fiend about privacy. Why do you think he moved from LA all the way out here to the country?"

A few minutes later they arrived back on the patio, leaving dirty footprints wherever they walked. Micah snagged a roll of paper towels from the kitchen and they wiped their feet.

"Let's have a hot shower, and then we'll figure out what to do next."

"Do you mind if I shower alone?" Jasmine asked.

She crossed her arms around her naked breasts, and wouldn't look at him. His heart sank and he wondered if she regretted what they'd done.

"Sure, no problem. You go shower first and I'll clean up the kitchen."

Jasmine glanced around at the mess. "Are you sure you don't want me to help?"

He shook his head. "No, you'll only distract me, and I mean that as a compliment, by the way."

As Micah led Jasmine through the bungalow to the master bathroom, he struggled to keep his eyes off her naked, muddy body.

"What about our clothes?"

"I'll throw them in the washer while you're gone. In a few hours, they'll be dry and good as new."

When he got back to the kitchen, he picked up their dirty clothes, took them to the laundry room, and tossed them into the washer.

He thought about his conversation with Jasmine during dinner and frowned as he scrubbed down the now-cool grill.

He understood the reasons why Lucy wanted to transfer ownership of the restaurant to Jasmine, but from the look on her face, it was clear she wasn't sure if she wanted to take it on.

His final decision was all the more difficult and pressing. If he did open his own restaurant, as his business partners preferred, he would now be in direct competition with Jasmine, rather than just her grandmother.

That didn't sit well with him, especially now.

Making love to Jasmine had changed everything.

She also seemed to have open disdain for his brother, which surprised him. Micah thought Gregory had a good relationship with the townspeople. After all, they'd elected him to a second term in office, rallying around him when his opponent tried to step into his shoes.

He knew that Lucy had even hosted a couple of town meetings at the restaurant for Vanessa, who at that point was not Gregory's wife, but his campaign manager. Was Jasmine even aware of the role, though small, her grandmother's restaurant had played in the election?

Jasmine hadn't been living in Bay Point for long. He wasn't sure how involved she was in local politics, but she probably wouldn't have such a negative opinion of her brother, if not for Lucy.

It was too soon to consider making Jasmine a permanent part of his life and his family, but Micah would never want a difference of opinion to tear them apart. If she was going to be part of his life, she and Lucy would have to come to grips with the fact that Gregory would be making some decisions about Bay Point they might not agree with.

His phone beeped and he read a series of texts from Zack. Inwardly, he smiled, but wondered how Jasmine would take the news. He laid his phone back on the counter and silently thanked the weather gods.

Micah chuckled out loud at his change of heart, realizing that he was closer to wanting a serious relationship with Jasmine than not wanting one. Something he never expected to happen so soon.

After he finished scraping the plates, he wrapped up the garbage and took it to the bin on the outside of the patio. He loaded the dishwasher and thought about the role he could play in his brother's plan to continue to revitalize the local economy.

His restaurant would bring much-needed jobs and more dollars to Bay Point. His name recognition and personal brand would help to sustain both through fickle economic times. Plus, it would help promote the Langston family name, which was important to his mother and father.

As he wiped down all the surfaces, he worried about Jasmine and whether continuing to keep his plans a secret was the right thing to do. The nondisclosure agreement that he'd had everyone who was aware of or involved in the deal sign was now hampering him. He couldn't even hint at his plans until he and his business partners made the final decision public.

"I wish I could tell her the truth," he said aloud.

Jasmine entered the room, body wrapped in a towel.

"Tell me what truth?"

"I—I just got a text from Zack," he sputtered, surprised to see her so soon.

Didn't women normally take hours in the bathroom?

He threw the paper towels in the trashcan and washed his hands again.

"I was debating whether to tell you or not."

She gave him a curious stare. "What's wrong?"

Micah braced his palms on the dining counter. "The heavy rains caused a rock slide on Highway 1. No way we're getting out of here tonight."

"What about another route?"

"There are reports of flash floods on the PCH, plus local roads nearby. It's not safe."

"Did you plan this?"

"Everything but the rain." He grinned. "And the rock slide."

He reached across the counter and took her hand. "I didn't know how you would react to the news, but the truth is, I'm not sorry we're stuck here."

Her brow creased in distress and she slipped her hand from his. "What am I going to tell Lucy?"

"She doesn't know that you're with me, does she?"

Jasmine shook her head. "I'm sorry, I didn't want her to know."

Micah clenched his jaw. This confirmed his suspicions that Lucy really did have something against the Langston family. Why else would Jasmine have to hide the fact that she was going to spend time with him?

He grabbed a throw blanket from one of the chairs and wrapped it around her shoulders.

"Will you excuse me? I want to take a shower, too."

She nodded and he gave her a quick kiss before he left to take a shower.

The hot water felt great, but didn't ease his tension or his hurt feelings. Though he was curious about the reasons why Jasmine felt it was necessary to hide their relationship from Lucy, he knew better than anyone not to get involved in family disputes.

Fifteen minutes later he was back, squeaky clean with a towel around his hips and ready to pick up the conversation where they left off.

"We might as well make the best of our time together, even though you don't even want to be here."

"That's not true," she cried. "I do want to be here and I want to be with you."

He sat down on the couch and patted the seat next to him. "I think I've made it pretty clear how much I want to be with you."

She sat down and her voice turned shy. "Thank you for the wonderful meal. I'm sorry we didn't get to finish it all."

He caressed her cheek with his hand. "Are you really sorry? Because I'm not."

Her skin was so soft that he didn't ever want to stop touching her. Luckily, he was able to keep his desire for her under control. For now.

Jasmine tilted her face, her mouth turned down at the corners. "Only that I was such a poor cooking student. I let you do all the work."

He paused his movements. "That just means you'll need another lesson."

She didn't smile, and he could tell her mind was elsewhere. He dropped his hand from her face into his lap.

"What's wrong, Jasmine?" he asked, suddenly tired, but wanting nothing more than to make her happy.

"I'm afraid the restaurant won't survive without Lucy's guidance, if I take it over. She works so hard. If something happens to her..."

Her voice trailed off and there were tears in her eyes.

Micah took her in his arms, and she leaned against him. "Shhh... Nothing is going to happen to Lucy. You said yourself that she is in good health."

She seemed to accept his answer, even though he had no way of predicting whether Lucy would get sick.

"Don't worry, whenever I'm in town," he continued. "I can give you a cooking lesson, no problem."

Despite his cheerful tone, her face crumpled a little, like she was hurt. But why should she be, he reasoned, hugging her tightly. She knew he didn't have a permanent residence in Bay Point. He wasn't going to tell her that his feelings for her had deepened. Not until he'd had a chance to explore them further.

Micah snapped his fingers. "Oh, I almost forgot something. Wait here."

He got up, grabbed his phone and texted Zack to ask where he'd hid the surprise he'd mailed to him. After he'd retrieved it, he went back into the living room and gave her a white box, wrapped with a red ribbon.

Jasmine's face lit up. "Presents, already? You really know how to get to a girl's heart."

She opened up the box, and pulled out a luxurious white cashmere robe.

"Oh my goodness, it's beautiful."

He stood and grabbed her hand, pulling her up with him. "It will look even better on you."

She let her towel drop and he whistled at the sight of her beautiful body. Micah knew at that moment that he would never get tired of looking at her. His control waned, and his cock stood at attention.

Jasmine dipped her eyes low and pursed her lips in a way that made his chest tighten.

"On second thought, this can wait."

She put the gift box and the robe on the couch, and then pushed him down next to them. He yelped in surprise and then groaned as she straddled him.

"But I can't." Her voice was a mere whisper, but her intent was clear. "Can you?"

Jasmine tapped her forehead to his as she positioned herself above him. He lifted his hips to meet her, but she kept herself just out of reach.

Micah threaded his fingers through her wet, curly hair. He could feel her heat and saw the passion in her eyes.

"Not a chance, baby." He gulped hoarsely as her body slowly swallowed him whole.

Chapter 8

Jasmine glanced over at Micah, at his hands gripping the steering wheel, his determined face. Was it possible to fall in love with a guy just by the way he looked when he was driving? Or the way he made love to you?

No, falling in love took a whole lot more, she decided as she turned away and stared out the window. It had to, because she couldn't pinpoint the second or the hour, or even the reason she'd fallen in love with Micah.

But she had.

It had started raining again, and she appreciated that he drove the convertible with care. Eyes straight ahead, serious. Not playing now, not like last night, she thought, a slight smile on her face. But he was serious then, too. About pleasing her. Over and over again.

* * *

The car wound along cliffs with multimillion-dollar homes perched on top. The expanse of the Pacific Ocean led westward to countries she'd never been before, and might never get a chance to visit.

She didn't need world travel. She needed Micah by her side, always.

Yesterday had been incredible, and not just the sex, although that had far surpassed even her wildest expectations.

The lunch he'd prepared, the wine they'd drunk and shared, the smell of the wet grass and sodden earth, the way he made her body feel.

Protected, cherished, revered.

Caring for her pleasure first, then his. There was still so much they had to discover about each other.

For dinner, he taught her how to make a homemade pizza, topped with prosciutto and mushrooms. It turned out so good she hoped she could convince Lucy to add it to the menu, in addition to her desserts.

After they ate, they spent the rest of the evening curled up on the couch watching movies. She in her luxuriously soft robe, he in his white cotton briefs.

They'd also talked a lot about Lucy and the restaurant. Micah seemed genuinely concerned and willing to help. That surprised her, given that his brother the mayor hadn't lifted a finger, although she wasn't sure Lucy had even asked. She didn't know what the mayor could possibly do to save the troubled restaurant. He could at least try.

She'd stopped short of mentioning the money they

owed to Mr. Stodwell, the landlord, as well as the back taxes they were struggling to pay. According to Lucy, the Langston's owned some of the buildings downtown, but not theirs.

Maybe that was a good thing, she thought bitterly.

Gregory would probably kick them out, and then raze it and build something new. Growing up in post-Katrina New Orleans, Jasmine had an innate distrust of politicians that wasn't likely going to change.

Later that night, they'd crawled into bed and Micah had made slow, sweet love to her, until she writhed and wept in his arms. Then they both fell into a blissful sleep. Waking up next to him was a continuation of a dream she hoped wouldn't have to end.

He touched her knee, and she jumped a little. "You okay, Jasmine? Want me to turn on some music?"

She looked over and smiled. "No, I like the quiet. It feels cozy with the rain pelting against the roof."

Micah glanced over quickly and nodded. "Like us under the blankets. I'm sorry I had to get us up and out."

"Back to the real world," she said, with a trace of sadness that their time together was over. "There's no escape, I guess."

"Depends on whom you're with," he replied, with a sly smile.

Jasmine was silent for a moment, and then said, "There is something you can do for me."

"Name it, and it's yours," he said with a snap of his fingers.

She turned in her seat to face him. "I want you to ask

your brother what kind of business is going in across the street from Lucy's."

His brow furrowed. "I thought you said you were hoping for a grocery store. What do you think might be going in?"

"That's the problem. Lucy and I don't know, and it'll be better if we do, so we can stop worrying and plan ahead."

"That place could stay empty for months."

"True, but I'd rather know sooner than later."

"I understand," he said, looking over. "I'll do what I can, but Gregory can be pretty tight-lipped when he wants to be."

"To the detriment of the people," she suggested.

Micah pulled off the exit for town. "That's a matter of opinion. I'm not around enough to stay tapped into Bay Point politics."

Jasmine touched his arm. "Maybe you'll think about sticking around?"

"I don't know."

Her heart sank when he didn't elaborate, but she figured he was merely concentrating on getting her home safely.

He pulled into a parking spot a few doors down from the restaurant and she was silently relieved. She'd called Lucy the night before to let her know that she wasn't at the beach, but rather with Micah.

Still she didn't want to call attention to the fact that she'd lied, nor did she want an audience at what she hoped would only be a temporary goodbye.

"When will I see you again?" she asked, taking care to keep her tone casual.

"Like I said a few minutes ago, I don't know."

His voice wasn't sharp, but there was an edge of resignation to it that made her press her back against the door.

Micah reached for her hand, held it, and she relaxed a little.

"We had a wonderful time. Let's leave it at that for now. Okay?"

"Fine," she said, snatching her hand away. "Then I guess I won't wait for you to call."

Willing away tears, she picked up her tote bag and purse from the floor and got out of the car, knowing he wouldn't follow her.

After entering the restaurant, she stopped in her tracks and hitched in a breath. Though it was the lunch hour, the place was only half full, the first time that had ever happened since she'd arrived.

This isn't good.

Jasmine hurried over to Donnie, who was clearing one of the booths on the far side of the wall, near the bar.

"Where is everybody?"

Donnie nestled the dishes in his plastic tray. "That new burger place is running a two-for-one lunch special. Lucy's jerk chicken is getting a beat down."

Though he probably meant his statement to be funny, neither of them was laughing.

"Where's my grandmother?"

He pointed a thumb upward. "Since we're so slow, she decided to take a break."

"I'm going upstairs to drop off my stuff and talk to her. I'll be back down soon."

Jasmine passed through the kitchen, said a quick hello to Gloria and walked up the back stairs to the apartment.

Her grandmother sat in an overstuffed armchair in the living room, a colorful afghan draped over her knees, reading a magazine.

She dropped her things next to the sofa, and curled up at Lucy's feet. "I'm sorry for lying to you."

"I appreciate the apology, but it's not necessary. You're a grown woman with your own life."

"I know, but I didn't want to worry you."

Lucy waved her concern away. "I've been more worried about you being stuck here with me. I'm glad you were able to get out and have some fun."

Fun? I wish it were that simple.

Tears sprang to Jasmine's eyes and this time she let them fall. "Micah is a really special man."

Lucy set the magazine aside and handed her a tissue. "If that's the case, then why are you crying?"

She closed her eyes and lifted her chin. "Because I don't know what to do. I don't think he feels the same way."

"Do you know that for sure?" Lucy asked.

"No, but he didn't ask to see me again," she sniffled, waving the tissue in the air. "Didn't ask me for another date. He just dropped me off."

Lucy stroked her hair, and Jasmine wondered if she was curious why it was now curly instead of straight.

"I never married, but I've listened to plenty of men

in my restaurant over the years. If they get too close to a woman, too fast, they run, even if they don't want to."

"It's so damn wrong," Jasmine huffed, and then blew her nose. "Even if he doesn't want to talk to me, he'll have to anyway."

Lucy waggled a finger at her. "Don't ever chase a man, Jasmine. You'll regret it."

"I'm not chasing," she protested. "I just asked him to find out from Gregory who purchased the building across the street."

"You shouldn't have done that," Lucy palmed her forehead. "I don't think I want to know."

Jasmine got up and stretched a cramp out of her left leg. "We have to find out. The dinner crowd is way down, and now lunch today. We have to be prepared."

"I know, dear," Lucy replied, her voice sounding worn out. "I shouldn't bury my head in the sand, but sometimes I wonder if it's time to let go."

"No, Lucy," she urged, sitting down on the chair next to her. "This restaurant is your namesake. You've devoted your whole life to it."

"Yes, but although I want to turn it over to you, I'm not sure if I want you to have the same fate."

This was her chance to tell her grandmother that she wasn't sure about her future in the restaurant business, or in Bay Point, for that matter. She was still mulling things over, and there were a lot of unknowns, like her status with Micah. She couldn't disappoint Lucy just because she didn't know what to do with the rest of her life.

Jasmine swallowed hard. "My fate *is* in my hands,

while *yours* seems to be at the mercy of Mayor Langston. I'm all for attracting new businesses into town, but he should think about the ones that have been here all along."

"Don't fault Gregory for what's happening. He takes after his mother, Helen, who has always felt a great deal of civic responsibility. But sometimes, he doesn't always show it to the people who need it most."

Jasmine leaned her elbows on her knees. "Regardless, we can't give up. We have to change with the times, and I'm going to help us do just that!"

Her grandmother smiled. "I admire your spunk. That's exactly the kind of energy I need for my business, and why I need you."

She smiled back and squeezed her hand. "We'll get through this, Lucy. With, or without, the Langston men."

All the way back to the estate, Micah wrangled with his thoughts. The way he had left things with Jasmine was not ideal. He should have gotten out of the car, walked her to the door and kissed her goodbye.

But instead, he'd let her go.

Everything was out of whack, out of sync, and he was quickly running out of time.

Micah pulled into the garage and walked into the kitchen. They'd woken up late and only had coffee before leaving the winery. Ginny had the day off, so he'd have to cook lunch himself, which, with his travel schedule, was something he rarely had the opportunity to do.

Immediately, his mind went to Jasmine and all the promises he'd made last night. More cooking lessons, helping her to develop new menu ideas and, he gasped aloud, a chick-flick movie night.

What a man will sacrifice when he's in love.

He stopped, the freezer door wide open.

Was he in love with Jasmine?

The possibility made him stare at a family-size bag of frozen asparagus like it was the Land of Oz.

Something inside him clicked, and his mind was clear.

A new roof and repairs to the exterior of the building were nearly completed. The electrical had been brought up to code; and a new water tank and heating and cooling system would be installed the following week. Liza Marbet was submitting her designs to him and his partners tomorrow. After one was selected and permits secured, Society Red could be open in as little as forty-five days.

After a deep breath, he pulled out his phone and sent his partners a quick email.

From now on, he would be the source of many problems and sleepless nights for Jasmine and Lucy, but there was nothing he could do about it. The decision was made, and there was no better way to deal with the guilt, than to meet it head on.

Though he was afraid of his feelings for Jasmine, he didn't want to completely turn away from them. If he did, he would likely regret it for the rest of his life.

Opening up his restaurant would allow him to be close to Jasmine and continue to get to know her. How they would co-exist as competitors and lovers in the same town he didn't know, but he aimed to find out.

Now all he had to do was tell her the truth.

A flock of seagulls crossed overhead, as Jasmine and Marlon jogged along the Pacific shoreline.

"I'm not supposed to even be here with you."

"What are you talking about?" she said, wiping the sweat from her brow.

Running on the beach was tough on the legs, but it was the best way to quickly build endurance and strength. Exactly what she would need if she hoped to complete the half marathon she was training for in a couple of weeks.

"My brother banned me from running with you. Can you believe that? He told me he was your new running partner."

Jasmine blew out a disgusted breath. "How can he be if he's never here?"

"True," Marlon said with a little pant. "I don't think Micah could keep up with you, anyway."

A knowing smile crossed Jasmine's face. She recalled how they'd moved together on the grass, the couch and in bed, challenging each other to deepen and lengthen their mutual ecstasy. Thinking of those times with Micah buoyed her heart and put her in a very good mood, despite not having heard from him.

"Where is he anyway?" Jasmine asked, hoping her voice sounded as casual as her stride.

She didn't know how much Marlon knew about her

involvement with his brother, and so she decided to act as if they weren't in a relationship at all.

"Mom said he's been in New York. I'm not sure when he's expected back. He rarely informs the family about his plans."

"Secretive man, huh?"

Marlon nodded. "He can be, but what guy isn't?"

Jasmine laughed, despite her inner worry. If Micah was keeping secrets from his family, what kind of secrets might he be keeping from her?

They jogged up the stairs on the side of the cliff, parted ways, and Jasmine headed back to the restaurant.

She guessed Lucy was right. Micah was doing his own kind of running, but hopefully not into another woman's arms.

A couple of weeks had gone by with no word from him.

It was like he'd dropped out of sight, much like the workers on the building across the street. The exterior had been repainted and new windows had been installed. The paper was gone, and when she'd looked inside, the space was stripped bare, down to the studs in the walls.

Jasmine still didn't know what type of business would be residing across from Lucy's. City Hall was a five-minute walk away, but because Gregory was Micah's brother, she didn't feel comfortable going over his head to get the answer. There had to be a reason why he hadn't contacted her.

Any mention of the space resulted in stress for her

grandmother. They'd find out soon enough. The building couldn't stay empty forever.

In the meantime, Jasmine stayed busy. Her life didn't revolve around a man. Never did, never would. Even though she missed him so much it hurt.

The decline in lunchtime patrons had turned out not to be a fluke. If Lucy wasn't concerned, Jasmine was worried enough for the both of them. She was finding it difficult to sleep, and when she wasn't thinking about Micah, she was researching other restaurants and menu ideas. Jasmine hadn't gotten up the courage to tell Lucy that the entire menu needed a revamp and needed to include healthy options, too.

Breakfast remained their most popular dining time, likely because they were the only option in town for a hot meal that wasn't fast food. Ruby's Tasty Pastries was too small to hold many customers and didn't serve hot food at all. Lucy's pancakes and chicken and waffles were favorites of many townspeople and tourists, but Jasmine couldn't bank on anything staying the same.

Lucy was still pressuring her to go to her lawyer, so that she could sign over ownership of the restaurant. Though she hadn't spoken about permanently shutting down, Jasmine knew that was still an option.

Jasmine continued to spend time with Gloria in the kitchen, learning how to prepare all the dishes on the current menu, and her skills were improving. She still felt nervous about cooking Lucy's famous jerk chicken because the ingredients weren't an exact science.

She checked her smart watch as she climbed the stairs to the apartment. There was just enough time for a quick shower before Lucy opened the restaurant at 7:30 a.m.

Her grandmother got up at 5:00 a.m. every day, and she and Gloria prepped for breakfast. Although Jasmine had offered to help, Lucy had declined, insisting that she take time for herself. On days she didn't run, she would either do yoga in her room or catch up on the stack of novels on her bedside table.

Life with her grandmother was pleasant, if not somewhat monotonous. After her time with Micah, she yearned for more excitement.

It was just after seven-thirty when she got downstairs and there were already a few customers in the dining room. Maisie and Liza waved her over to their booth. She hadn't seen them since the dessert taste-testing event.

"Good morning, ladies! What can I get you?"

Maisie gave her a broad smile. "My usual, chicken and waffles." She turned to Liza. "What about you?"

"I'd like to order five coconut cakes."

"Did I hear you correctly?" Jasmine gasped, one hand cupped behind her ear.

"Yes, but not for me," Liza responded, laughing. "I have five new clients, so I'm going to give them each a cake as a welcome gift."

Jasmine sank down into the booth in disbelief.

"Congratulations! I hadn't thought about selling my desserts outside of the restaurant."

Liza frowned. "Oh, but you will bake them for me, right? I was counting on you."

"Of course," Jasmine said, quickly. "It's just such a surprise."

"Why do you act so shocked," Maisie asked. "We all told you how delicious everything was that day. Didn't you believe us?"

"I did, but I guess I didn't believe in myself," she confessed.

Maisie patted her hand. "Honey, this is living proof that your baking deserves more attention."

As of right now, Lucy had only agreed to add her Triple Berry Crumb Crust pie to the dinner menu. Maybe this would pave the way to more of her desserts being served.

"I guess you're right, Maisie."

She turned to Liza. "I'll be happy to make the cakes for you."

After they discussed timing and delivery, Liza left for an appointment. She put Maisie's order in and came back with a pot of coffee.

"Sit with me for a moment," Maisie urged. "It gets lonely by myself sometimes."

Though she had work to do, Jasmine nodded.

She poured two steaming mugs, before setting the pot down. She added a little cream to hers and took a sip.

"Where's your beau?"

"Prentice?" Maisie pursed her lips. "Working as usual. Sometime I think that man loves his post at City Hall more than he loves me!"

Jasmine smiled. "Any news from the mayor's office?"

"If you like turning yourself into a human pretzel, I hear there's going to be a new yoga studio in town."

Jasmine laughed. "I enjoy the meditative qualities of yoga, but yes, some of the poses are challenging."

"Try impossible for a woman of my age," Maisie retorted. "Lord A'mighty, I hope Mayor Langston doesn't turn Bay Point into a hipsters' retreat. Some people can pay twelve dollars for a burger, but I can't."

Keep prices affordable.

It was obvious, but she made a mental note anyway.

Some of the recipes she was considering had exotic ingredients. Anything that drove up costs would have to be passed on to the customer, and they couldn't risk losing more. It was a delicate balance, and if she ever saw Micah again, she would ask him how he dealt with the issue.

"Trust me, I can't either. Have you heard what's going into the building across the street?"

Maisie shook her head. "No, but they did a wonderful job preserving the historical integrity of the building's facade didn't they?"

Jasmine had to agree with her on that point. "Even the new windows are quite attractive."

Maisie gave her a conspiratorial wink. "Plus, I can finally peek into them! Though I don't have a clue what it's going to be."

"Don't you think the businesses that are already here have the right to know who's moving in next to them?"

Maisie looked up to thank Donnie, as he set her plate before her, and then back at Jasmine.

"I know it's hard, but I have to believe that Mayor

Langston is doing the best he can for this town. It's not easy trying to please all of the people, all the time."

"It's impossible, I imagine," Jasmine said.

"And it's not for us to know everything, all the time." Maisie patted her hand and laughed. "Not even me."

Though she did not agree, Jasmine smiled politely. "You're right. I've got to get back to work. Enjoy your breakfast."

The rest of the day went quickly. That night, after a hot bath, she checked her phone. Her breath caught in her chest as she listened to a voice mail from Micah, inviting her to join him in New York City for a couple of days.

Jasmine tossed the device on the bed, excited to see him again. The timing was bad, but there was no better way to find out if the feelings she had for him were real.

Chapter 9

Micah gazed out of the floor-to-ceiling windows and twiddled his thumbs behind his back. Taxis and trucks, small as ants, inched bumper-to-bumper down the traffic-clogged road. He barely noticed the carpet-like autumnal beauty of Central Park's trees spread out as far as the eye could see.

He should feel like a king.

But without Jasmine at his side, he was quickly discovering how empty his world was, and had been, for a very long time.

He'd spent the last couple of weeks in meetings with his agent and his production company, as well as builders, suppliers and employees. Everybody wanted something from him.

Not Jasmine.

The edges of his lips lifted into a smile.

All she wanted was his body and he didn't have a problem with that at all. But if she wanted his heart and to share his future, would he be so willing?

The thought of giving his life to one woman made him feel like he was choking. He tugged at the collar of his shirt and then loosened his tie.

Jasmine could never accuse him of making promises. Since their time at the winery, he hadn't called her. It was to her benefit that she hadn't called him, either.

Though he wouldn't admit it, he was testing himself.

Even when he couldn't stand being away from her any longer and had invited her to New York, she hadn't said yes immediately. Gave him the "I have to check my calendar" bit.

But in the end, it didn't matter that she'd made him wait three days for an answer. She was on her way and would arrive any minute.

His lopsided world would be right again.

He turned away from the window and walked over to the phone. His apartment was undergoing renovation, so he'd booked a room in a luxury hotel. Everything must be perfect, he thought, as he ordered room service. The flight from California was long and he knew that Jasmine would probably be tired.

Flowers. Dinner. Candlelight.

All should help to stem the effects of jet lag, and hopefully, get him and Jasmine back on track.

To where, he wondered, as he plopped into a chair. He stared at the last text message he'd received from Jasmine.

Can't wait to see you.

He wondered if she would feel the same way once he told her that he was the one who not only owned the building across the street from Lucy's, but was weeks away from opening up a restaurant there.

In one way, he knew that he was taking a huge risk inviting her to New York, only to let her down.

But he had made a commitment to his business partners and to his brother Gregory that he would honor, even if it broke Jasmine's heart.

Micah stretched out his legs and leaned his head back to wait. Due to all the traffic, he wasn't sure when she would arrive, but it wasn't long before he heard several knocks at the door.

Opening it, his eyes widened in surprise and he hardened with desire. He wanted nothing more than to swoop her up in his arms, lay her down on the bed and kiss her all the way into tomorrow.

"Hi!" Micah flushed at his simple greeting, but that was all he could muster.

Although Jasmine was casually dressed in a pink V-neck sweater and black jeans, she might as well have been wearing an elaborate ball gown.

He wanted to kiss her, but held back unsure of how she would react. He took her bag and gestured for her to enter the room, hoping she could not see the growing bulge in his pants.

She nodded her thanks and made a beeline straight to the windows. He wasn't offended, as he'd done the same thing earlier.

"Gorgeous, isn't it?" he remarked. Only he knew that he wasn't talking about the view.

The sweater clung to her body, hugging the curves in her skinny jeans in a way that made a permanent stamp on his mind. She kicked off her strappy gold heels and they landed near the bed.

Her toes curled into the plush beige carpeting, as if she was trying to gain purchase.

"We're so far up."

Her voice breathless with awe, she swayed in place and he swore she was going to faint. He looped his arms around her waist and pulled her toward him.

"I've got you."

She leaned against him and sighed. It took everything in his power not to rub his tight length against her tight bottom. Her lips parted and he knew that she could feel him pressed against her, and how much he wanted her. A few seconds later, she stepped away and he stifled a groan.

"It's beautiful."

She started to turn around, so he loosened his grasp, but didn't let her go. If he had it his way, if he could put life on hold, he would never let her go again.

"But I still prefer the view of the ocean to this."

Micah put his fingers to his lips and looked around surreptitiously. "Shhh. Don't let a New Yorker hear you say that or you and I might not make it out of town alive."

Jasmine laughed. "It's just that when I see all the buildings, it seems like everything that could be accomplished has already been done. But when I look at the ocean, it's a blank slate of possibilities."

Though her rationale made sense, he didn't care what was outside the window at the moment. He only cared about her, and the chance he was about to take.

Micah pressed his lips together, wondering whether it made sense to tell her the truth now. His lips moved to her neck, pulsing and throbbing against its gentle curve.

Tilting her head to the side, she moaned and melted back against him. He inhaled a whiff of her perfume, dark and syrupy sweet, like the taste of skin.

"I've missed you, Jasmine."

Words whispered into her ear collapsed into a deep sigh as she turned and flung her arms around his neck. Mouths smashed together, they slowly sank to the floor in a tangled heap of unbridled desire with tongues that wanted nothing but to devour.

Micah wasn't the type of man to take anything without asking, but when Jasmine broke away and yanked her sweater over her head, all he could do was reach, and pull, and finally, suck.

She giggled out loud and whipped the remnants of her bra from where it had caught on her arm. It hit the window and slid to the floor.

Seconds later, she was moaning with him, grinding against him. He closed his hands around her bare waist and slipped them around front, not bothering to unbutton her jeans.

It was the challenge of the deep dive, moving his hand down toward a warm, wet place, known only to him. Palming the coarse hairs, tickling the twin crevasses of smooth flesh. The joy of finding his treasure warmer and wetter than he'd initially expected was the reward for his effort.

Jasmine halted further exploration with a smile, as she undid his belt buckle and slid down his zipper with her teeth. After removing the rest of her clothes, she sat back and watched as he struggled to remove his pants.

"This is one view I'd never get tired of," she purred.

She stroked his penis jutting like a wild sentinel through the gap in his boxers. Her grasping and pulling motions on his flesh made him want to howl.

He started to undo his shirt, but his fingers froze on one button. Her smile was demure, but what she was doing to him was anything but innocent.

Jasmine seemed intent on destroying his resolve to maintain some level of control, and he loved her tenacity. Loved the way she pumped her hand faster and faster, her eyes dark with heated determination.

The sensual sight of Jasmine's mouth closing over his penis was too hot to bear. Micah heaved a loud sigh and tore at his shirt, ignoring the buttons that took to the air like birds released from a cage.

He groaned all the way to the floor. Lying flat on his back, he stared at the ceiling. Though it was white, he saw colors, as innumerable pleasurable sensations tumbled through his lower half and spread throughout his body.

"Baby, you better stop," he said, haltingly.

All of a sudden, he heard some furious knocking at the door, but that didn't deter Jasmine. She moaned, him in her mouth, licking him into near oblivion.

"Who is it?" he shouted, clenching his abdomen as Jasmine's hands cupped and gently massaged his swollen sac.

"Room service," a cordial voice responded.

"Leave it outside, please," he yelled, lifting his head up to watch her pleasuring him.

Now on all fours, she placed her palms on his abdomen and stared into his eyes as she slowly released his painfully hard cock. Jasmine was so beautiful that he felt tears smarting in his eyes, as he panted slow breaths.

When she ran her tongue over her glossy wet lips, Micah almost lost it. He got up on one elbow and with his other hand, tilted her chin up with his finger, not trusting himself to speak.

For a moment, he was embarrassed at his emotions. Before he knew what was happening, she mounted him. He strained to lick at one taut nipple, but she wouldn't let him and pushed him back to the floor.

She consumed him fully with a loud moan, and immediately began to rock slowly, back and forth.

"Oh, god," he croaked.

The pressure to explode inside her was agonizingly sweet. He cupped her bare buttocks, holding on, bringing her as close to him as he could get without melting into her.

It was the only control she would give him.

This woman, *his* woman, was tight. A wet, warm flower yet to bloom.

Her hips danced and stroked, and Micah swallowed hard, watching her move. Not missing a beat, she leaned over and kissed him, her tongue moving inside his mouth.

Before he could return the favor, she was upright again. Breasts bouncing, nipples hugely erect, head thrown back as if he were merely a guest in her pleasure-filled world. Her loud moans, melding with his, seemed to reverberate throughout the room.

They crushed and swiveled their perspiring bodies together in a whirlwind of motion that he never wanted to end. When Jasmine began to pant uncontrollably, he grabbed her hips, knowing she was close to breaking through the erotic haze they'd created together.

As she slid down his flesh, he dug his heels into the carpet and ricocheted his pelvis up to meet her in a deep, penetrating jolt that caused her to gasp aloud. As he emptied his soul inside her, she closed her eyes and bit his shoulder to muffle her screams.

"Was that better than an ocean view?"

Jasmine lifted her head from Micah's chest and blinked her eyes open in disbelief. Their frenzied love-making had mellowed into a strange silence, and she was relieved that he had spoken first.

"If I say yes, can we do it again?" she teased.

His smile reached his ears. "Of course. I guess that means you don't mind staying in for the night?"

She shook her head. "As long as you and I are together."

He slapped her butt, and reluctantly, she rolled off his body.

"I guess I'd better get the food. I'm starved."

She sat cross-legged and watched Micah pad into the bathroom. A few minutes later, he came out with a towel wrapped around his waist and a robe in his hand.

As he helped her into the garment, a sense of peace washed over her.

Micah kissed her cheek. "Are you okay?"

She nodded. "Yes, just hungry. I'm going to wash up while you get everything ready."

Alone in the bathroom, she peered at herself in the mirror. Her cheeks were flushed and the glow in her eyes wasn't due to the lighting.

It was time to admit that she was in love.

She turned on the hot water tap and the steam rose, clouding her reflection. After rinsing out her mouth, she cleaned her face and her body with a wet washcloth. Though she wasn't ashamed of what they'd done, she knew she wouldn't be able to eat if she felt sticky and sweaty.

Still, she couldn't rid him from her heart, nor did she want to. He was lodged there, a reminder that sometimes being able to sink into someone else made all the stress and worry disappear. At least temporarily, she mused, as she slipped back into the robe.

Jasmine stepped out of the bathroom and held in a gasp. A round table was in front of the window, complete with a white tablecloth, china plates and silverware. A bottle of wine served as the focus between two pillar candles.

Micah turned toward her and smiled. "The food is still warm, thank goodness."

He lifted the silver domes off the plates and set them

on the desk nearby. After that, he poured two glasses of wine and they settled into their chairs.

They enjoyed an easy banter throughout the meal of kale salad with apples and pine nuts, New York strip steak with baby red potatoes and carrots, and chocolate cake for dessert.

Jasmine devoured it all, plus two glasses of wine. She sat back in the chair, thoroughly stuffed. “Everything was delicious. It’s like you already knew what I wanted.”

“I do know what I want.” His voice turned husky. “I want you.”

Tears filled her eyes. “If that’s true, why didn’t you call me? Why haven’t I heard from you?”

Jasmine clenched her fists, afraid that she’d lost control of her feelings for Micah. She didn’t bother to disguise the hurt she’d been holding inside ever since their night at the winery.

“I mean I’ve got to fly all the way to New York City to find out what’s going on with us?”

Micah folded his arms and stared at her. “Is that the only reason why you came here, for an answer?”

She shook her head. “No, as if you couldn’t already tell, I missed you.”

“I think we’ve both proven how much we missed each other.”

A smile twitched at the edges of his mouth. “I didn’t call you because I didn’t want to pester you. I know you have a lot on your mind.”

“Yes. I’m very worried about the restaurant. Lucy still wants to hand it over to me, but I’m not ready and

I don't know if I ever will be. She's even threatened to shut it down permanently, because she doesn't want it to be a burden to me."

He got out of his seat, took her hand and led her to the couch. "Then let me help you."

Jasmine bit her lip. "How?"

Micah pulled her into his arms. "Tomorrow I want to bring you to my restaurant and show you how I do things."

"But Lucy's is tiny in comparison to Society Red."

"Yes, but there are certain ways to run a business that apply no matter what the size."

Jasmine tilted her head. "That's true. I know there are some things that I want to change from a marketing perspective to attract more customers."

Micah nodded. "If you're going to bring more people through those doors, you want to make sure you're ready."

A warm glow spread through her at the concern in his eyes. "I'd appreciate any help you can give me, but what about us?"

He grinned. "I'd hoped you forgotten about that thread."

Jasmine fumed inwardly. Why did men always try to avoid talking about relationships? Was it built into their DNA?

She flattened her hand on his chest. "Not so fast, buddy. I do have a brain with this body."

Micah stroked her hair and his tone sobered. "I know you do. I didn't mean to offend you."

She couldn't help but melt inside, because she knew in her heart that he hadn't meant to hurt her.

"I just want to know where I stand," Jasmine said, taking the blunt route.

He took a deep breath. "We're getting to know each other slowly in a way that matters only to us. There's no timeline here."

She bit her lip, wondering if no timeline also meant no commitment. She'd been down that road before, although in hindsight, it was a blessing that she'd never pursued something permanent with her exes. Maybe a wait-and-see approach was actually a good thing because it left space and a chance for true love.

Jasmine nodded. "I agree. We're both very busy, but I'm afraid that I won't see you that often. I know that you rarely come home to Bay Point."

"Now I have a reason." She frowned and he continued in a hasty tone. "Not that my family isn't important, but they will always be around."

No they won't.

Jasmine thought of her grandmother, who was getting up there in age. She was one of the most important people in her life and Jasmine knew that she had to help ease her burdens. Doing so would help Lucy enjoy the fruit of years of hard work while she still could.

She gazed up at him. "Do you think I'm the type of woman to sit around waiting for a man?"

His eyes grew large. "Are you kidding? I'm not going to let you go long enough to find out."

Jasmine slipped her arms from her robe, letting the garment pool around her waist. Her body warmed as she watched Micah's eyes spark with renewed desire. She shoved the robe onto the floor and climbed onto his lap. His hardness throbbed against her side, and he groaned trying to adjust his body. But she pressed against him, imprisoning him, wanting him inside her and soon.

"Make love to me, Micah," she whispered, nuzzling at his jaw, now rough with stubble. "Make love to me so I'll *want* to wait for you forever."

He scooped her up and carried her over to the bed.

He spread her legs with hands hot as fire, and penetrated her slowly, prolonging the moment, inch by delicious inch, until he could go no deeper. Tears sprang to her closed eyes as Micah's lips found hers.

In the middle of the night, Micah woke up with Jasmine in his arms. He slid one arm out from under her and she turned onto her side, but stayed asleep. It had been a long time since he'd wanted a woman as much as he wanted Jasmine Kennedy. There was something about her that made his mouth salivate, not just with desire, but to know her, inside and out.

He put his hands behind his head and stared at the ceiling to avoid pulling her toward him again.

What am I going to do? His words were silent, but his mind whirred with a mixture of excitement and worry.

The fact was there wasn't anything he *wouldn't* do for Jasmine. Except give up his restaurant.

He couldn't lose her. Not now, not when everything seemed to be just beginning, with every kiss and every touch. And somehow he knew that it would always be like that, because that's the way he wanted their relationship to be. Always fresh, always new, always on the brink of something wonderful, even in the midst of unspeakable joy.

Yet, he felt stuck, too. In the sin of omission, he dwelled in a safe space of his own making. Telling Jasmine the truth could destroy everything they were building together. He knew she wanted a relationship with him, even if she wouldn't admit it.

It also surprised him how easily he could see her being a long-term girlfriend. Maybe even his wife.

Whoa, he muttered to himself. *Slow down.*

But lying to himself would be fruitless. He was falling in love with Jasmine, and it seemed his feelings deepened every minute he was with her.

Waiting to tell her the truth would be better, he reasoned. It would buy him some time to woo her, to make her his own. He would not only be her lover, but also a business mentor of sorts. Nobody held the trade secret to success. He would give her as much advice as she wanted, but it was up to her to apply it to Lucy's.

And when he opened up his restaurant, she would quickly find out the meaning of competition. Despite his feelings for Jasmine, he had a duty to his business partners and to Gregory to make a profit.

He would wait, he decided as he lightly stroked her hair, and make her love him as he already loved her.

She lifted her head from the pillow and his breath caught in his throat. Feelings he couldn't express rose in his heart and threatened to burble to his lips.

"Micah? Is everything all right?"

Her voice was sexy with sleep, and he felt his body

stir with primal need, a gut-wrenching desire he knew would never go away.

Micah turned over and spooned against her, his penis so hard it hurt. But in her sleepiness, she didn't notice, which made him want her even more.

"Everything's fine, baby," he whispered.

Though her body was warm, he drew the covers over their shoulders, and then cupped one of her breasts in his hand. Her nipple remained soft as velvet against his palm, and he bit his lip to stop himself from stroking it, molding it, until it would be as hard as he was.

With a ragged sigh, Micah kissed Jasmine's mussed-up hair and eventually fell back to sleep.

Chapter 10

Jasmine crossed her legs and slid her feet into a more comfortable position under her chair. Micah had invited her to sit in on a meeting for the third season of *High Stakes Chef.* The coffee contained in the heavy white porcelain mug with Magnum Vice, the name of the production company, emblazoned on it had long since grown cold.

So had her interest in the proceedings.

Fifteen minutes of fame, be damned. Not that he'd asked her to appear on *High Stakes Chef.* If he did, she would refuse and take her desserts with her.

The conference room, located on the forty-fifth floor of an office building on Lexington Avenue, was nondescript. The long wide cherry wood table, where deals were made for the lucky and hopes dashed for the unlucky, was shined to a high gloss. There was no art on the walls, but the place didn't need it. It was the unobstructed views of the iconic Chrysler Building that drew the eye.

Sitting around the table were two key members of the team. She'd long forgotten their names but she'd never forget their faces.

The director had a suntan-leathered face that had once been handsome. His blue eyes were shifty, always somewhere other than where they should be. A few times they'd landed on Jasmine, sizing her up in a not-so-subtle way, and she'd looked away. He made her uncomfortable and she wished she'd had the guts to walk out, but she didn't want to cause trouble for Micah.

The other participant in the room, Micah's producer, was attractive, with a brutal laugh. She had a pixie cut, a long nose, and pursed her lips as if she had a torrent of ideas just waiting to burst forth.

Micah was busy looking up at the large screen television, instructing the show runner to make changes to the script.

"We can't forget the picky eaters in our audience," he instructed.

"Or the thrifty ones," the producer said.

How about the ones that are bored, she thought and crossed her arms.

"Write whatever it takes to boost ratings," the director barked.

Jasmine felt a laugh burble up in her throat and before she knew what was happening, it spilled out.

"I thought they only said that line on television."

Micah turned and smiled, however the reaction from his production team ranged from shock to amusement.

"It's statements like that which make it clear why nonindustry people, or outsiders, should never be invited to meetings like this," the director growled. "Why is she here anyway?"

Micah raised his palms midchest. "Calm down. This is my show and I can bring whomever I wish to these meetings."

She had no idea how popular Micah's show was, but he'd confessed last night that he enjoyed the challenge of the format. She'd also realized that filming, held in a Brooklyn warehouse, would keep him away from Bay Point for weeks at a time.

The closer she got to him, the more she was falling in love with him. How would it feel to let him go, to trust that he would stay faithful to her, no matter in which city he happened to lay his head?

He clasped her hand and brought it to his lips in a show of support that melted her heart, but not the tense mood in the room. Micah must not have noticed, or didn't care, because he didn't let go as he addressed the team.

"Our ratings are fine. We're popular with our viewers and even though we're on hiatus right now, we're gaining even more through social media outreach and streaming video sales."

"Otherwise, the network wouldn't have renewed us for another season," the producer asserted, in an obvious attempt to suck up. "I'll get you my ideas for the set by the end of the day, Micah. I think some slight modifications would allow our live audience to be more interactive, instead of mere stooges for applause."

Micah nodded, released Jasmine's hand and turned toward the screen, addressing the show runner.

"Please make the changes we discussed and email the revised script back to me this afternoon."

He stood and pushed his chair back. "Let's go, honey."

Ignoring the people who didn't want her there anyway, Jasmine took one last look at the Chrysler Building.

She looped her satchel over her right arm and with Micah on the other, swept from the room, feeling like a queen.

As soon as the elevator doors closed, they burst out laughing.

"I'm sorry, Micah." She hiccupped and covered her mouth with one hand. "I didn't mean to sound rude. I hope I didn't embarrass you. I didn't realize creative people could be so touchy."

His broad smile deflected her sudden guilt, and opened up her heart to the possibility that this man had a very forgiving nature. That was good, because sometimes she would need it.

He leaned one shoulder against the elevator wall. "Don't worry about them. They'll get over it."

By the time the elevator got to the first floor of the building, they were packed in like toys on a shelf at Christmastime.

They exited onto Lexington Avenue, and Micah

pulled her to the side of the building. She looped her hands around his neck and gave him a kiss.

"Where to now, superstar chef?"

"Are you still up to lunch and a tour of Society Red?"

Without answering, she ran to the curb and stuck her hand out to hail a cab. Seconds later, one pulled up.

Micah strutted to the curb and opened the door before she could. "I guess that's a yes." He laughed, guiding her in.

"Battery Park, please," he instructed the cabbie.

The taxi jolted away from the curb and merged into heavy traffic. Jasmine grabbed Micah's hand as the cab swung around the corner, barely missing a few pedestrians. She looked back, horrified, but the people continued on their way as if they hadn't noticed.

She leaned her head on Micah's shoulder. "Are you sure we're going to make it there alive?"

"Don't worry, I'll protect you," he said, his deep voice, low and sexy.

Jasmine shivered as he nuzzled his cheek against her hair. For once, the thought of a man protecting her didn't feel wrong or old-fashioned. It felt like love.

She glanced up and was startled to see that he was already staring down at her. The desire in his eyes was unmistakable as he trailed a finger along her jaw.

"I'm really glad you're here," he said. "The day feels different."

"Different?" she repeated, arching a brow. "How so?"

He looked up at the ceiling of the taxi, searching for words.

"Brighter. Sharper." He leveled his gaze on her and smiled. "And a little less crazy."

She rolled her eyes and sighed. "Being the normalizing factor in your life sounds so boring and unromantic."

"There's not a boring bone in your body. And as far as romance, you've inspired me to think that it still exists."

"Really," she said, genuinely intrigued. "I didn't know guys cared about romance."

He tapped his finger on the tip of her nose. "That's because you haven't been with the right man."

Jasmine hitched in a breath. "How do you know you're the one?" she asked, putting the last two words in air quotes.

"Let's see." Micah wedged his chin in between his thumb and forefinger, as if in thought. "I'm handsome. I can cook, and I know the proper way to handle a knife and fork."

He turned, eyes roaming lightly over her body, and she elbowed him in the side.

"Don't you dare!" she warned.

"What did you think I was going to say?"

His wide-eyed innocence made him look even more handsome.

"That a man is only as good as his mind?"

Micah pinched his fingers together. "Close. Try again."

"A man is only as good as a good woman next to him?"

"Bingo," he affirmed and gave her a quick kiss. "You and I have a lot to learn about each other."

She snuggled against the crook of his arm, thrown lazily across her shoulders, and her tone turned serious. "Are you sure you can handle me?"

She was surprised when he looked down at her with concern. Maybe he was more tuned into her feelings than she thought.

"I—I think so, but your voice sounds like maybe I won't. Care to tell me why?"

"I'm not the type of person to take chances," she blurted.

"Then you probably shouldn't be in this cab," he joked.

She shot him a look and slid away. "I'm not kidding, Micah."

He frowned, and Jasmine knew that she'd made her point.

"Okay, I'm listening."

"I'm a very rational person," she continued. "Which means that I don't often do something without putting a lot of thought into it. I don't know if it's engrained in me, or something I picked up from my father."

His smile was encouraging. "You haven't talked much about your family. I've been wondering about them."

She exhaled, not sure why she hadn't confided in him before, but she was ready to now.

"There's not much to tell. My parents are from very humble backgrounds. They divorced when I was twelve years old. I never really asked why, but I think it was because my dad, who runs a small boutique hotel in the French Quarter, was too complacent and too logical. I think my mom was just bored."

"How do you know?"

"Both of them were very private, meaning that I couldn't really tell how they felt about each other. I never saw them kiss, never saw them hug."

He shrugged his shoulders. "I'm not sure that's so unusual. Many parents don't show their affection for each other around their kids."

"It is when you have a mom who can't stand not being seen. She loves being the center of attention, whereas my father and I are quite content to remain quietly in the background. Sometimes I wonder if my mother became a teacher so that she would always be in the front of the room."

"What grade does she teach?"

"Second. And all the kids adore her." Jasmine paused and frowned. "I guess my dad and I were never enough for her."

"Is that why you dropped everything to move from New Orleans to Bay Point?"

"Yes." She nodded, and then quickly shook her head, thinking of her former boss. "I mean, no. My grandmother needed me."

"Was she sick?"

"No, just tired. And I needed a change."

Jasmine bit her lip, and debated how much to tell Micah about the real reason she left home. But after all that they'd shared together so far, she knew it was time to take a chance on the truth.

"I left, not only to help my grandmother, but because I also needed the work. I'd recently gotten fired from my job."

Micah raised a brow. "What happened?"

"One night, we were working late on a pitch. My boss made a pass at me that I refused to reciprocate. So he fired me on the spot."

"Did he hurt you?"

She shook her head, and watched Micah clench his fists.

"That bastard. I wish I would have been there to protect you," Micah said, his tone heavy with regret.

"Me, too," she said.

"I have zero tolerance for sexual harassment anywhere, but especially in my workplace, and I make sure all my employees know it. I've had to let a few go because of that type of behavior."

Jasmine was impressed that Micah had taken such a strong stance.

"What happened to me was unfortunate, but it also gave me a reason to leave New Orleans and not look back. At first, I thought I was running away, but now I realize I was running toward my future."

She poked her finger into his chest. "And I ran straight into you."

He grinned. "Are you sure you don't want to run back?"

If I did, would you care?

Jasmine shook her head and smoothed a lock of her hair back into place. "I'm not sure. There's something about Bay Point that enchants me."

He frowned, as if he were upset that she didn't take the bait. "What attracts you that I don't know about? I grew up there and couldn't wait to get out."

"How about its history of attracting Hollywood actors and actresses? Lucy said the town used to be filled with them."

Micah shrugged. "That was a long time ago. I never saw any stars when I was growing up, but Gregory told me he has had some recent interest from production companies looking to film there."

Jasmine clapped her hands. "That will be great for local businesses, including ours." She stopped when Micah made a face. "What's the matter?"

"The town is in such a state of flux right now. A movie production could actually hurt us, not help us."

She raised a brow. "I'm surprised to hear that coming from a big TV star such as yourself."

"Who knows what can happen when things go wrong on a set," he interrupted.

"You sound as if you're speaking from experience. Have you ever been caught in your dressing room with a contestant from your show?"

He burst out laughing. "That's a wild example, but no. My reputation is too important for me to lose it. I don't like to take chances, either."

She smiled. "I guess we're more alike than I thought."

"I would never hurt you intentionally, Jasmine."

He looked deep into her eyes, like he was about to say more, but they'd arrived at their destination.

Micah paid the cabbie and they got out. As the car drove away, Jasmine's eyes followed it.

"Anything wrong? Did you leave something in the back seat?"

"Only my privacy," she replied. "I just realized we had a very personal conversation within inches of another human being."

Micah slipped his hand into hers and grinned. "Welcome to New York."

After the tour and lunch, Micah had wanted to spend the rest of the day with Jasmine. When he suggested they do some sightseeing, she announced she wanted to explore South Street Seaport on her own. So he took a cab uptown, disappointed because he'd hoped to talk to her and find out what was going on in that beautiful mind of hers.

Ever since they'd walked into the doors of his restaurant, Jasmine's mood had taken a turn for the worse.

It wasn't anything that she said or did.

She'd listened intently as he walked her through the reservation software, which made it easier for patrons to book tables online. She seemed impressed with the ordering software that made it seamless for his staff to enter meal choices and helped his operations team keep track of inventory.

She oohed and aahed at the top-of-the-line equipment in his kitchen, and at the orderly flow of the meals from prep to cooking to plating.

Instead of pleasing him, her compliments made him nervous. With all her talk about not wanting to take chances, he wondered if she was having second thoughts about him.

A few months ago, he would have welcomed an open opportunity to leave her without guilt. But now, he knew it would devastate him if he could never see her again.

Deep down, he knew his love for her was growing stronger.

It was her independence that attracted him the most. She may not need a man, but he was quickly realizing how much he needed her. If he'd learned anything since they'd met, it was that sharing his business knowledge and his bedroom would never be enough for him.

He wanted to share his heart and his life with her.

Micah opened the window, and caught the glare from the cabbie in the rearview mirror, but he didn't care. At that moment, he felt as though he couldn't breathe.

Something else occurred to him.

Maybe Jasmine was having second thoughts about owning her grandmother's restaurant. That would make it easier for their relationship to succeed beyond the lover zone.

Lucy would be forced to sell the restaurant to someone else. He wouldn't have to worry about the effects his restaurant's success would have on Jasmine.

He knew she would never completely abandon her grandmother, but what would she do if Lucy's closed? Would she go back to New Orleans?

She'd talked about a catering business for her pies and baked goods, but was that sustainable in a town as small as Bay Point?

As far as he knew there were no advertising or marketing agencies close by, so she wouldn't be able to get the kind of job she'd had in her hometown. He supposed he could hire her in a marketing role, but feared she would be offended if he offered.

Besides if she didn't want to be with him, she wouldn't want to work with him either.

Micah got out of the cab at 57th and Madison, and headed west toward Fifth Avenue. A few minutes later, he stepped through the doors of Tiffany & Co.

Although greeted warmly by the store employee, he frowned. He needed to think about what he was about to do.

No, he told himself, he needed to stop thinking about it, and just do it.

Micah forced his feet to walk toward the back of the store, where he took an elevator up to the second floor.

A salesperson approached him almost immediately.

"Chef Micah?" Upon his nod, she continued. "I thought I recognized you. Can I help you with something?"

He frowned again, though he appreciated that she'd lowered her voice. He assumed his privacy would be held in the strictest confidence. He couldn't take a chance that his purchase would end up shared over social media.

"Is there somewhere I can shop without being around all these people?"

The woman nodded. "Certainly, follow me."

She led him to a private salon, where he told her what he was looking for and she scurried off. He hoped she would hurry up so he wouldn't change his mind. Fifteen minutes later, she returned and slid a tray of glittering diamond rings onto the counter, and he broke out into a cold sweat.

"I'm just browsing," he insisted, as much to himself, as to the clerk.

She gave him a knowing smile as she extolled the virtues of carat weight, cut, color and clarity of each ring. She didn't bother to ask him if he could afford it, and he didn't bat an eye when she told him the price of each one.

He was too busy trying to calm his heart, which pounded in his chest as if he were about to skydive from an airplane. Something he told himself he would never, ever do.

He reminded himself that he also said he would never, ever get married. Now he was seriously thinking about it.

"Who's the lucky lady?"

"I'll let you know when I find her," he replied, deciding to play it coy.

Micah held up a ring at eye level, all five carats of glittering beauty in a platinum setting.

It was as perfect as the woman who would wear it.

Maybe wear it, he corrected inwardly.

His phone rang, and he saw Gregory's name on the screen.

"I'll take this one."

He handed the ring and his credit card to the saleswoman.

She nodded. "I'll get it wrapped up for you."

When she was gone, he caught the call.

"What's up, bro?"

"You tell me," Gregory countered. "I'm hoping for some good news."

Micah thought about the ring, and wondered if he should confide in his brother, but quickly squashed the idea. It would be better for both of them if he kept their conversation strictly business.

"You win," he said.

"Does that mean—?"

"Yes, Society Red will be opening in our dear town in less than a month."

"Well, all right brother!" Gregory exclaimed. "Where are you? What made you change your mind?"

Micah hitched in a breath, not trusting himself to speak. He'd tried to keep his emotions out of the decision, but he'd be lying if he didn't admit that Jasmine had played a significant role.

"New York City," he said. "Earlier, I had a meeting with my production team, but right now I'm at Tiffany."

Gregory chuckled. "Are you scouting locations? I can't imagine how management would feel about you rolling a couple of giant grills down the aisle."

Micah replied in a dry tone, "Ha-ha. Stick with your day job."

"So you're not going to tell me what you're doing in the most famous jewelry store in the world?"

"Nope."

"Does Jasmine know you're there?"

"Ditto, and she's not going to find out."

"So you've finally come to your senses. It's about time. You need a good woman who will give you a reason to put your wheels down and stay in one place for a while."

"Maybe I came in here to get out of the cold," Micah replied.

"Yeah, right," Gregory snorted. "And someday I'm going to run for president. When will you be back in Bay Point?"

"Soon. I have a few more details to work out here."

"Does she know about Society Red?"

"I'm going to tell her tonight."

Micah hung up a few minutes later. The salesperson slipped into the room and handed him his credit card receipt. He glanced at the price, paused and then signed. She gave him a Tiffany gift bag with his purchase inside, and left him alone in the room.

He sat there for a while, his heart racing with excitement over the decisions he'd made. Though the future was still uncertain, Lucy and Jasmine's life was about to change, and soon everyone in town would know it.

Chapter 11

Jasmine tightened her seat belt as she listened to the pilot announce that the plane would be landing in ten minutes. Curling her hand behind her neck, she attempted to massage the knots out of it, but the problem wasn't stress. It was worry about what might be waiting for her when she got home.

Earlier that morning, she'd been asleep in Micah's arms when she received a call from her grandmother. Alarmed, she grabbed the phone from under her pillow and swiped it on.

"There's something you need to see," Lucy said right away, dispensing with her usual pleasantries. "Please come home as soon as you can."

She asked if Lucy was sick and was relieved to hear that she wasn't. Jasmine knew better than to press her for more details. She just got out of bed and called her airline to see if she could change her flight.

She wasn't supposed to be coming home until the following day, but Lucy needed her. Although she hated to leave Micah, in Jasmine's mind, family always came first.

The plane eased through the white, billowy clouds on its descent into San Francisco International Airport. Even though she was aware of the principles of aerodynamics, the study of forces, of motion, lift and drag, there was still something otherworldly about flying.

It was kind of like being in love, she thought. The heart soars to unfathomable heights and all you can do is hope that once the clouds fall away, you don't take a nosedive, but instead land in one piece.

Jasmine popped a stick of gum in her mouth, closed her eyes and tried to ignore the baby fussing behind her. At that moment, she wished she'd had the courage to ask Micah if he wanted children. They hadn't discussed their future, and maybe they would have, if their time together hadn't been cut short.

And though he promised they'd see each other soon, it bothered her that he wouldn't nail down a specific date or time. Jasmine didn't believe that absence made the heart grow fonder. In her case, absence from Micah made her heart just ache.

Tears sprang to her eyes and she chided herself for not telling him how she felt when she had the chance. She knew he didn't want her to leave, and she was grateful he didn't ply her with questions she couldn't answer anyway.

Jasmine smiled at the memory of the night they'd shared. Micah had taken her to a Broadway play, and then an intimate dinner in the West Village. After returning to the hotel, they drank expensive champagne that tickled her nose and made her laugh as they soaked in a hot bubble bath.

The playful preamble turned into a long, lovemaking session that turned her inside out. As he brought her to multiple orgasms with his lips, his tongue, and his slow and easy thrusts, she wanted to cry out how much she loved him. But she held her feelings locked away, even as she begged him for more.

They'd fallen asleep, her on top, him still inside her, just before dawn. Jasmine squeezed her thighs together, remembering how he'd filled her inside, the exquisite pleasure he'd given her.

How she missed him right now, and she knew that her longing for him would only get worse. Just thinking about his taut, muscular body and the way his skin felt under her hands made her almost go crazy with sexual need.

She took a deep breath and exhaled slowly, forcing herself to relax.

The time she'd spent with Micah in New York City had been magical, but would it always be that way? She could see herself married and having children with him, but they'd discussed none of those options, perhaps because they didn't want to break the spell they'd both had a hand in creating.

Jasmine knew that it was important to come down from out of the clouds and land in a reality of their very own. It remained to be seen if they could be a full-fledged couple, without sacrificing their individual dreams.

Thirty minutes later she stowed her bags in her car and began the long trek home. Bay Point was a ninety-minute drive from the airport, so she wouldn't be there until nightfall.

It was after six o'clock and the rush hour traffic was slow and heavy. After two connecting flights and eight hours in the air, she was bone tired and starved.

Before getting on the PCH, she got a couple of cheeseburgers and a large soda to go. Normally, she didn't eat a lot of junk food, but there was no time for a sit-down meal. She had to get home to find out what was going on with Lucy.

Jasmine devoured her meal and tried to groove to her favorite contemporary jazz station, but the soulful rhythms reminded her too much of Micah, so she turned the music off.

The questions she'd never asked him seemed to gnaw and pick at her brain against the background of silence. She stuck her hand out of the open window, her fist clenching and releasing, as if she could capture the answers in the air.

"I'll tell him that I love him," she vowed.

And if he didn't feel the same way, then there would be no need to delve any deeper. She could stop hoping for a long-term relationship and consider him as a lover, moving on when, and if, she met someone else. The problem was that he'd captured her heart, and right now, she wasn't sure she'd be able to release it to another man.

By the time she got home, the sky was streaked with dark pink and gold. After stowing her bags upstairs, she grabbed her half apron and tied it on. Despite the unknowns, she was excited to get back to work.

She found her grandmother behind the bar serving customers, and gave her a hug. Though she'd only been gone a few days, Lucy seemed thinner and frailer than she remembered. It saddened her, but also strengthened her resolve to find out what was going on.

"Need any help?"

"No," Lucy shook her head. "I'm glad you've arrived safely. Did you park in back?"

"Yes, of course. You told me to always leave the spaces up front for customers. Why?"

Jasmine pressed against the back wall as Lucy squeezed by her.

"And what was so important that you couldn't tell me over the phone?"

"Follow me," Lucy said. "I need to show you something."

The dining room was nearly empty as they weaved around the tables to the front. Jasmine raised a brow as they went outdoors, but nothing had prepared her for what she saw across the street. For the windows now emblazoned with the Society Red logo.

She stood openmouthed, not believing what she was seeing, until she crossed the street for a close-up.

A few moments later, Lucy was at her side. She

cupped her hands, and without touching the window, peered inside.

"Chairs and tables are in. The place looks like it's going to open soon."

Jasmine traced the lettering with her eyes and her stupidity became as clear as the glass. Her heart broke at Micah's obvious display of deceit.

Lucy touched her shoulder, and she jumped.

"I take it that he never told you."

She gulped back tears. "I can't believe it. This was his restaurant the entire time."

Lucy nodded sadly. "It appears so. I guess you can figure out why I couldn't tell you on the phone."

"Why didn't you?" she demanded.

"I wanted you to see this for yourself. So when the time comes to confront Micah, you can react with a rational mind, not an emotional one."

Her face warmed with embarrassment, and then shame that she'd been taken in so easily by Micah's good looks and charm. She stared through the glass and her voice shook as she spoke.

"I know what I want to do right now. I want to throw a brick through every one of these windows. That's how angry I am."

She crossed her arms and huffed out a breath.

"He even took me on a tour of his location in New York. He's been trying to help me, giving me tips on how to improve our operations. Why would he do that?"

"I've never claimed to understand human motivation," Lucy replied. "But I'm really surprised that he didn't let you know. Even though their father is an ambulance-chasing lawyer, all the Langston men are typically very honest. Or at least, they were."

"What are we going to do?" Jasmine exclaimed. "I'm not sure if you know this but Micah has a history of running other restaurants around him out of business. And we're unlucky enough to be right across the street!"

"We were here first."

Under the subdued glow of the streetlamp that had just flickered on, her grandmother's lined face looked fierce, rather than tired.

"Sounds like you're ready for a fight," Jasmine observed.

"I just want to save what I've worked hard for my entire life."

Jasmine draped her arm around Lucy's thin shoulders and squeezed gently. "I'm ready to help you any way I can."

Lucy patted her hand. "Thank you, sweetheart. I knew I could count on you. Now we better get back. It's almost closing time."

Later, back in the apartment while Lucy took a shower, Jasmine unpacked her bags and threw a load of laundry in the washing machine.

Micah had left a voice mail earlier, checking to see if she'd arrived in Bay Point. Instead of calling him back, she texted that she was home and very tired. She left it open as to whether they would speak soon, or at all.

Her throat ached from the need to cry, but she refused to give in to her feelings. What would be the point, she thought as she stowed her suitcases in the back of her closet. She wouldn't need them anytime soon. No more impromptu trips to New York for a man who couldn't even be bothered to tell her the truth.

She knew she couldn't avoid him forever. He'd pointed out during the tour that from an operational standpoint, his restaurants didn't require his involvement day-to-day. Though she had no idea how often he planned to be in Bay Point, she assumed he'd be around a lot more, at least initially.

Mired in thought, she headed into the kitchen and made a pot of herbal tea. Although she was exhausted, she wanted to stay up a little longer and think of a plan that would help Lucy fend off the competition, from Micah and other new restaurants in Bay Point.

She stared at a business card stuck behind a magnet on the refrigerator, then took it and smiled. After pouring herself a cup of tea, she went into her grandmother's bedroom and handed her the card.

"Are you sure?" Lucy asked, patting the side of the bed.

"Yes," she said, sitting down. "I'm ready to take the next step."

Lucy smiled. "I'll call the lawyer in the morning to make it official."

Jasmine kissed her goodnight on the cheek and left the room. She was proud of herself for taking a burden from her beloved grandmother and placing it on her own shoulders.

Her steps felt lighter and more purposeful than ever, but her heart remained broken.

Micah held back the urge to lay on his horn as he inched along behind a row of cars on Magnolia Avenue.

Outside his rolled-up window, Bay Point's downtown sidewalks buzzed with activity.

The streetlamps were wound in yellow crepe paper streamers. Kids held onto red and white balloons, and hop-skipped ahead of their parents, laughing and pointing. Stores displayed their wares, and people milled about, talking and browsing.

He rubbed his palm over his eyes, and released the brake to inch up a bit more. All he wanted was a parking space. He'd already checked the alley in back of his restaurant, and there were none available.

While he waited for traffic to move, Micah made a mental note to tell his construction manager to post no-parking signs so that he'd have a better chance of having a spot whenever he was home.

He wanted to surprise Jasmine, so he didn't tell her he was back in town. Nor had he told her about the restaurant as he'd planned to do in New York. There never seemed to be a right time to broach the subject, and he didn't want to spoil even one second of their moments together.

Now he had to tell her the truth and he needed the conversation to go well. If it didn't, he would face whatever consequences ensued, and hoped they wouldn't be too disastrous.

The grand opening was in two weeks, and even if he could postpone it, he would not. The wait staff and cooks had been hired, and he'd sent invites to his friends in Hollywood and the culinary world.

A car pulled out from the left-hand side of the street and he slammed on the brakes. The vehicle had just enough room to squeeze into the line of traffic, and as soon as it was safe, Micah pulled into the vacated parking spot.

At the sight of his restaurant logo on the window, his brief exultation turned to dismay and his heart sank.

"What the hell is that doing there?"

The logo wasn't supposed to go up until a couple of days before the grand opening. Then he wondered how long it had been there. No question Jasmine had seen it, or if not, she would soon.

All of a sudden something caught his eye in the rear-view mirror. He turned and glanced behind his shoulder, half expecting to see Jasmine at the door of her grand-mother's restaurant, but it was only a customer exiting.

Micah turned back, relieved, and called his construction manager. When he asked how long the sign had been up, his fingers grabbed hold of the steering wheel when he heard the words *over a week*. Too shocked to argue, he thanked him and hung up.

"Arrgh!" he grit out, frustrated.

The error was likely due to miscommunication on someone's part. Who exactly on his team was to blame he didn't know, but it hardly mattered now.

He ran a hand over his hair, knowing what he had to do next, and got out of his car before he lost the courage.

The traffic had eased somewhat, but he still had to wait a few moments until it was safe to cross the street.

At Lucy's, he tried to enter but the door wouldn't budge. A sign indicated the restaurant was closed. Cupping his hands, he peered into the window and saw Jasmine sitting at the bar, with her back toward him.

He knocked on the glass until she turned around and noticed him. Instead of the smilc he was expecting, she frowned and he knew that he was in for a battle.

She took her time getting to the door, her hips swaying with every slow step. His desire grew just by watching her walk, and he realized that she had a hold on him that would be devastating to lose.

When Jasmine opened the door, he gave her a sheepish grin.

"I guess you saw the sign."

He moved to kiss her, but she stepped back and crossed her arms.

"Ya think?"

"Can I come in and explain?"

With a shrug of her shoulders, she ushered him in and then locked the door.

"Why are you closed in the middle of the day?"

She slid into a nearby booth. "We always close after lunch, in order to prepare for dinner, which is a good thing because I have some decisions to make."

He sat down opposite her. "Any that involve me?"

"Everything is not about you, Micah." She blew out a breath. "But then again, maybe it is."

"What do you mean?"

"Look outside, would you?" Jasmine said, pointing toward the window. "I can't believe you're even asking me that question!"

The hurt look on her face made him close his eyes for a moment to say a quick prayer.

"Why didn't you tell me?"

He slid his palms faceup across the table hoping she'd

take the hint and put her hands in his. When she didn't, he folded them back together and knew he'd need more than prayers to get him out of this jam.

He'd need a full-blown miracle.

"I'm not going to say that I tried to, because I didn't." He paused and licked his lips. "The truth is, I was scared."

"You should be," she insisted, eyes flashing. "Just because we're a tiny restaurant doesn't mean you can swoop into town and destroy us. Not without a fight."

Micah sat back against the booth, half expecting her to reach over the table and throttle him. He grabbed a straw from the dispenser and unsheathed it from its paper, just to have something to do with his hands. "Just listen to me, okay?"

He could see the pain in her eyes, and knew there was a chance she would never forgive him.

"The building itself is owned by me and my business partners, who are also chefs and restaurant owners."

"Sforkin Industries?"

He nodded and she added, "I went to the city records office and that's all the information I could get, and when I did a search under that name on the internet, nothing came up. So, why did you decide to have your restaurant here, and not one of your partners?"

"Bay Point is not a very well-known city outside of Northern California. We decided that my restaurant would be better since I have more name recognition."

Micah swallowed hard, hoping he didn't sound as conceited as his statement.

"I assume the mayor knew, too?"

"Yes, Gregory and my entire family were under a nondisclosure agreement."

Jasmine tucked an errant strand of hair behind one ear. "Great. Now Lucy and I look like idiots in front of the mayor, too."

He slammed his fist down, angry at himself for putting her through this. She nearly jumped out of her seat and he immediately regretted the action.

"No, you don't. I'm the idiot. I should have been honest with you from the very beginning," he said more quietly. "I could have told you as soon as everything was decided."

"I guess I can understand the need for a nondisclosure agreement," Jasmine said, as she fiddled with the silverware. "But you still haven't told me why it was so important to keep the truth from me."

"I told you. I was afraid."

She pushed the silverware aside, and the jangling noise hurt his ears. "I have a hard time believing a famous chef would be fearful of anything other than food poisoning."

"I was afraid of losing you."

Micah stared at her, but she wouldn't meet his eyes, as his words hung in the air between them. He debated for only a minute, before he got out of his seat and slid in next to her.

He put two fingers under her chin and guided her face forward so he could look into her eyes.

"Don't you believe me?"

She shook her head, and her eyes were moist.

"How can I, Micah? You can't expect me to believe anything when you've lied to me for this long."

His fingers drifted to the table, as if pulled down by a heavy weight. He kept his gaze on hers, until her lips parted. He wanted desperately to kiss her, but he knew that now was not the right time.

"But it no longer matters," she continued and her voice sounded weary. "You'll be dealing with me from now on. Not my grandmother. I own the restaurant now."

In spite of the tense atmosphere, he smiled with pride. "I know that was a hard decision, but you'll do a great job, especially if you follow some of the suggestions I made in New York."

"At this point, I'm not sure if your advice is warranted, let alone, necessary."

He knit his brows together, frustrated at her tone, even though he understood that she wasn't happy with him. "If I wanted you to fail, do you think I would have been trying to help you all along?"

She massaged her temple with two fingers. If the wall between them could be seen and felt, Micah was sure it would be made of heavy grade steel.

"I don't know what your motivation was, and I no longer care."

She pressed her knee against his. Micah knew she wasn't flirting with him, but wanted him to move out of the way. He couldn't hold her prisoner in her own restaurant, so he reluctantly slid out of the booth.

"We're not finished," he said.

Jasmine held her chin high and looked him square in the eye as she opened the door.

"Yes we are. Thank you for telling me the truth, although it's a little too late. We're competitors now. Though I didn't realize it, I guess we always have been."

"I didn't come to Bay Point to hurt you."

Nor to fall in love, he added to himself, as he stepped over the threshold. But that was exactly what had happened. Telling Jasmine his feelings now would only make things worse.

Tears splashed down her face. "Oh really? I wish you'd never come home at all! I wish I'd never met you!"

She slammed the door shut. The closed sign swung back and forth across the glass like a pendulum, mocking him.

Chapter 12

Two weeks later.

Jasmine finished refilling a bunch of soda orders, free for all customers that day, and then nodded at the repairman as he edged through the swinging kitchen doors, toolbox in hand.

The air conditioning system had broken for the third time that week, and she cringed in fearful anticipation of the bill. Since she'd taken ownership of the restaurant, it seemed as though everything that could go wrong, had gone wrong.

In addition to the air conditioner, the dishwasher was on the fritz, too. Some of her suppliers had raised their prices, forcing her to start the search for new ones. Donnie, her longtime busboy, had quit and taken an assistant manager trainee position over at another restaurant. She'd taken over his duties, and continued to help with bartending and waitressing, too.

Worse, she and Micah weren't speaking. It wasn't his fault entirely. He'd called and texted her multiple times, which she ignored. She loved him, but wasn't ready to mend fences yet.

The repairman slid his invoice across the bar, a grim look on his face, and she gasped at the amount circled in red. It was higher than he'd quoted her when he arrived that morning.

"I had to get creative because the parts you need aren't made anymore. This unit is so old you'll save more money in the long run by replacing it."

She wiped the sweat from her forehead, and moved in front of the small fan she'd set up at the back of the bar.

"It'll start to cool down in here soon. Better shut those windows in front," he continued and dug a business card out of his shirt pocket. "I wrote down the model number of the unit I recommend. This company will give you a fair price, and they always have some in stock."

Jasmine took the card and stuck it near the cash register. "Thanks. I'll be in touch."

She put all the sodas on a tray, and worked her way around the restaurant carefully. As she distributed the drinks to each customer, she announced that the air conditioning was fixed and thanked them for their patience.

The room was starting to cool off, but she left the fans on to speed things up. As she shut the windows, she avoided looking across the street at Society Red, but sometimes she couldn't help being curious. Most of the work was going on inside, and she had too much pride to peek through the windows after dark.

The most important decision she'd made thus far was closing the restaurant for dinner. After doing some further competitive research, she discussed her findings with her grandmother and they decided it was best not to fight the inevitable.

By sticking to breakfast and lunch only, they could increase their profit margin over time, without having to worry about being decimated by Micah's restaurant, which was only open for dinner.

Jasmine put together a marketing plan, including a website, social media presence and a small advertising budget that would help attract new residents and more visitors. The decor could use some sprucing up, too. But those efforts took money.

She didn't want to take out a loan, but it was starting to look like she had no choice. She needed money for the air conditioner, dishwasher, plus the software and order management equipment Micah had recommended to bring Lucy's into the twenty-first century.

The breakfast menu would remain traditional; steak and eggs, pancakes and sausage, toast and jam. Lunch would continue to feature Lucy's famous jerk chicken sandwiches and other Cajun favorites.

Jasmine wanted to extend the menu, and she would love to go to San Francisco and visit some of the hot new restaurants there to get some ideas. But even if she could get away for a weekend, it would be strange dining alone. She'd rather have Micah there, to offer his opinion, but that was impossible now.

Maisie waved her over to her booth. "Sit down, honey. You look like you could use a break."

Jasmine set down three sweet ice teas on the table and plopped into the booth. "If one more thing breaks, I might just take a swan dive off the Bay Point Pier without a life jacket."

Maisie took a long sip and smacked her lips in appreciation. "Ah. The joys of being a small business owner."

Liza, who was joining her for lunch, fingered the droplets that had already formed on the glass.

"I guess I'm lucky in a way. I rarely have to deal with equipment breakdowns, other than the battery in my phone dying on me," she said.

"No, I'm the lucky one. You ladies have stuck with me these last couple of weeks, through all the breakdowns, including my own."

A few hours after Micah had left over two weeks ago, Maisie and Liza had stopped in to see how she was doing. Though she'd put on a brave face in public the entire time he was still in New York, her grief and tears over his lies came pouring out over a few glasses of wine with her newfound friends.

Maisie patted her hand and snorted in disgust.

"You've had a rough time. I'm still upset with Micah and Gregory. I can't believe they kept Society Red a secret, especially from me, and I know everything that's going on in this town."

"And I'm still sorry that I couldn't tell you, because

of that stupid nondisclosure agreement I signed," Liza added.

"I know it was hard to do, but you were right to turn down Micah's project, Liza."

"I'm glad I didn't sign with someone who can't be honest with the person he *claims* to love."

Maisie clucked her tongue. "Not so fast. If there's one thing I know about the Langston men, when they fall for a woman, they fall hard and true."

Jasmine was momentarily tempted to share her innermost feelings about Micah, but to do so, felt a little like betrayal.

Liza cleared her throat. "It worked out for the best though. I have more clients than I can handle right now, and—"

She patted her stomach and lifted her eyes shyly. "With a baby on the way I need to be careful about my project load."

Maisie and Jasmine looked at each other at the same time, and then squealed in unison. Some of the patrons in the restaurant glanced up at the ruckus, and just as quickly, went back to their food and conversations.

"Congratulations! Babies are always wonderful news!"

"We'll have your baby shower at the B&B," Maisie offered. "I'll take care of everything."

"Thank you!" Liza grinned. "Anthony and I are very excited."

"Much as I'd like to keep chatting, I'd better get back to work."

Jasmine started to slide out of the booth, but Maisie gently grabbed her arm.

"Have you seen him?" she whispered.

"No, not at all."

Maisie tsk-tsked and Jasmine accepted her motherly hug. "That's too bad. He'll come around."

She shrugged. "I don't care if he does."

Liza and Maisie looked at each other. "Yes, you do."

"That's my cue that break time is over." She gave her friends a tight, but warm, smile.

"By the way, lunch is on the house, ladies."

I don't care if I ever see him again.

That's what she told herself over and over again, as she rang up checks, returned credit card slips for signing, and began to clear the empty tables.

Perhaps if she said the words often enough, she would start to believe them.

"If Micah knew I was here, he'd have my head on the chopping block."

Jasmine rolled her eyes as she jogged with Marlon alongside the surf of Bay Point Beach.

"I assume you knew about his restaurant, too?"

"Of course, I did," he said, breathing lightly. "But I couldn't say anything because of the—"

"I know, I know," Jasmine interrupted, with a wave of her hands. If she heard the words nondisclosure agreement one more time, she would scream.

"Anyway, Micah is not stealing the tongs and taking over when I grill for the family, which to me, is the same as howling at the moon. He seems depressed. I get the feeling the man misses you."

"He does?" Jasmine asked, even though she knew what he was saying was likely true. Her lips lifted at the memory of their time at the winery, when he tried to teach her to cook, and ended up doing most of the work himself.

"Watch out!" she shouted, pointing at a beer bottle sticking up in the sand.

Marlon grunted as he barely missed tripping over it.

"Thanks. You sound like you don't believe me. Still mad at him, huh?"

She gave him a sidelong glance and stifled her annoyance.

"Why do men think women can get over being hurt as easily as they can?"

"Is that a serious question?"

"Yes, it is. I'm curious."

"I can't speak for all men, especially not my brother. But if it were me and I was truly sorry, I'd just want you to forgive me."

"Just like that?"

Marlon nodded. "Yep, and why not? What is the point of holding on to a grudge, especially when you love the guy."

Jasmine stopped in her tracks and put her hands on her hips. It took a few seconds for Marlon to realize she was no longer by his side, and then he stopped and walked back over to her.

"What did I say now?" He bent over and put his

hands on his knees, gasping for breath. "Whatever it is, can we keep going? We still have another mile."

Jasmine shook out her legs and jogged in place to stay warm. "Just answer me one question. How do you know I love him?"

"You think I haven't noticed how much you *haven't* talked about Micah for the past couple of weeks? You used to gab about him constantly, ask me questions about him. Funny thing is, he's asking me more about you than ever before."

She shook her head and took off running in the opposite direction, toward the pier.

He caught up with her moments later. "You know, when someone runs away, they're usually running from the truth."

Jasmine glanced over and huffed. "So what if I am?"

Marlon picked up his pace and she hustled to keep up with him.

"Someone has to stop running. Otherwise, how will you ever get back together?" he tossed over his shoulder.

Though his words made her mind pause, she kept going, trying to understand her fear of a reunion with Micah. She didn't know if he loved her, but suspected that he did.

However, a single goal now divided them: the survival of their respective businesses. His money, popularity and experience gave Micah the upper hand in that department.

If his restaurant hadn't moved in across the street, it would have been one of his partners'. She feared that her grandmother's legacy in town wouldn't be enough to attract new customers. She knew she couldn't count on the loyalty of her existing customers forever, especially if she didn't have the funds to make the necessary changes to keep them coming back.

She sprinted ahead of Marlon, wanting to be alone in her thoughts. Running as close to the waves as she could without getting wet, she realized how safe she'd been playing things with Micah. Competing with him scared her, but his fame did, too. She was afraid of losing a sense of belonging and importance in his eyes, and in his heart.

Jasmine wanted to feel involved in her man's life, but if they were constantly on opposite sides, how could she?

She glanced over at the waves and slipped off her shoes and socks.

Marlon caught up to her. "What are you doing?"

"I'm going for a swim. What else?"

"In your running clothes?" She nodded and he grinned. "Wish I could join you, but I'll be late to work if I do. See you in a few days."

She watched him jog away and when she was alone, stepped to the edge of beach.

The waves tumbled over and tickled her feet. She waded in slowly, the water deliciously cool, renewing her senses. The ocean swelled around her, and so did her determination to protect Lucy's legacy, and her own.

The grand opening is in less than an hour.

Micah felt a combination of wonder and disbelief as

he thought about everything that had transpired in the months since he'd come back to Bay Point.

His knees popped as he squatted down in front of the large, rectangular-shaped chalkboard near the hostess station. As soon as his life calmed down, he had to get back to the gym.

The last few weeks had been hell on his body. He was lacking sex, sleep and his one true love. Without Jasmine, he had none of those things.

I want her back, he thought, barely noticing his wait staff hustling around him, or the two pieces of chalk in his hand.

Everything was ready. The jazz trio, comprised of local musicians who were long-term friends of his father, were tuned up and ready to play. The fifty invited guests would be arriving at any moment and hopefully Jasmine would be among them. Since she refused to speak to him, he'd issued the invite for the grand opening directly to her grandmother.

Micah drew a large but lopsided heart on the chalkboard, and hitched in a breath, suddenly aware of what he had done.

He smudged it away with the heel of his hand before anyone could see, wishing it were that easy to erase Jasmine out of his mind. She was there constantly, in spirit, reminding him of how much he wanted and needed her.

Positioning his hand in the upper right-hand corner of the board, Micah eased the yellow chalk into a reasonably shaped circle, and colored it in. Then he took the orange chalk and drew long, squiggly lines to represent the rays of the sun, reflective of life itself.

The path to happiness is never straight, he mused often, but weaves forth like the curved roads of the Pacific Coast Highway. Beautiful, but dangerous if one drives too fast, and gone in a flash.

As he signed his name at the bottom left hand corner in bright blue, he hoped he hadn't ruined his chance at making things right with Jasmine. If she'd written him off, he couldn't blame her, although he had called and texted her several times.

As the days rolled by before the grand opening, it seemed as though his to-do list grew larger instead of smaller. He pushed her rejection aside, to the deepest recesses of his mind, and figured that it was probably better that she wasn't around.

But he knew that wasn't true either. Rather, he'd come to realize how painful it was to have the woman you love so close, literally across the street, but not be able to reach her in any way.

Micah hadn't given up trying to get her back. He'd just put his efforts on hold.

Finally, he stood. "Nobody can claim I'm a Leonardo Da Vinci."

"But you're a darn good chef."

Micah turned at the sound of his older brother's voice.

"Hey! I didn't hear you come in, but I'm glad you're the first to arrive."

Micah wiped his hands on a paper towel and went to jab Gregory in the side with his elbow. Gregory moved away just in time, and then gave Micah a brotherly slap on the back.

"Where's Vanessa?"

"She had to stop in at the shop for a few minutes."

Micah handed the chalk pieces to a server passing by, and then placed the board exactly where he wanted it.

"I can't thank her enough for the beautiful flower arrangements. She was right. They really add a nice touch to the tables."

In order to support the Bay Point economy, he decided to buy local as much as possible, including produce and flowers.

"What about Jasmine? Have you seen her lately?"

Micah shook his head. "Marlon has. He told me he's still running with her."

"That should be you by his side, not him."

"I know. I'm hoping she'll be here tonight with Lucy."

Micah frowned. "I wonder if Lucy told her that she and I are in cahoots together."

He wasn't going to reveal any details, but he and Lucy had a surprise for everyone that he hoped would go over well with the crowd tonight.

"Did you just say cahoots?" Gregory furrowed his brow. "Now I know you've been working too hard."

"Lucy's words, not mine."

He went and sat at the bar, knowing he'd be on his feet for most of the night. "Want a drink?"

Gregory waved the offer away and sat next to him. "So, you want to tell me what's going on?"

Micah sighed. "Where do I start?"

"How about with the truth? What are you going to do about Jasmine?"

He leaned his elbow on the bar. "Don't you worry, I've got a few tricks up my sleeve."

Gregory laughed. "Let's hope Jasmine doesn't make *you* disappear."

Micah joined in, and then quickly sobered. "If she shows up, I'll know I have a fighting chance."

One of his wait staff stepped into his line of sight.

"Chef Micah, can you come into the kitchen for a moment?"

"Uh-oh, that's not good. Will you excuse me?"

He instructed the hostess to show Gregory to the VIP tables that were reserved for his family, as well as Lucy and Jasmine.

Entering the kitchen, Micah found two employees arguing over the best way to plate one of his signature dishes.

After insisting that they follow the instructions exactly as they were trained, he told them that could present their ideas at a later date. Although he had a certain creative vision for his culinary dishes, it was important that all his employees see him as open and approachable.

Back in the main dining area, he greeted the guests that were starting to arrive.

Mixed in with his excitement about the festivities was growing anxiety about Jasmine. Every time the door opened and it wasn't her, his heart dropped. The doors were solid wood, so he wouldn't know she arrived unless he planted himself in front of the windows.

The dining room was almost full and he was starting to lose hope when, a few minutes before the appetizers were to be served, Jasmine walked in with Lucy grasping her arm.

Micah exhaled a sigh of relief and hurried to meet them. "My favorite two ladies in the whole wide world."

He kissed Lucy on the cheek, and she beamed with surprise.

Turning to Jasmine, his lips idled on her warm skin a little longer than proper in public, but he didn't care.

"We need to talk," he whispered in her ear. "Can you meet me back here later, when everyone is gone?"

She nodded, and he squeezed her hand gently before stepping back so the hostess could lead them to their seats.

Micah signaled to the bandleader to wrap up the tune they were playing, so he could make a quick announcement before the appetizers were served. When the applause died down, he cleared his throat and took the microphone.

"I'd like to welcome each and every one of you to the inaugural dinner at Society Red. The meal I've prepared for you is representative of the cuisine that I've spent years perfecting. I trust you will find every course delicious, but if you don't, please tell me. I welcome your opinions just as long you don't throw food at me like our esteemed mayor used to do when we were growing up."

Gregory picked up a roll from the breadbasket and with a grin on his face, acted like he was going to toss it on stage.

Micah pretended to duck and the audience roared.

"I want to give a special shout-out to the mayor for his leadership," he continued. "And his commitment to evolving Bay Point into a popular tourist destination, as well as a town that I'm proud to say is my hometown."

After the applause died down, Micah went on.

"At all my restaurants, I try to source as much as I can locally. This evening, I would like to recognize one person in particular. Ms. Lucy Dee Diller, who provided me with her jerk spices recipe, which I have modified to make it my own. My staff is standing by to serve you, so without further ado, let's eat!"

Micah watched Jasmine turn in shock to her grandmother and mouth the word *why*. But Lucy, who had a serene smile on her face, had entrusted him to explain everything to Jasmine, which is what he planned to do later on.

Micah knew she wouldn't say a word.

After the evening ended and the staff was gone, Micah texted Jasmine and asked her to return to the restaurant.

He didn't receive a reply, so he was on pins and needles as he waited for her, wondering if she would show up.

About thirty minutes later, there was a knock on the front door and he quickly ushered her in before she could change her mind.

"Did you enjoy the food?" he blurted out.

Her lips were pursed and he could tell right away that she wasn't happy.

"It was delicious. The compliments I heard throughout the evening were well deserved," she replied, in a perfunctory tone. "But I suppose you knew that already."

"Not necessarily, but thank you. I was hoping everything would go well. I was nervous."

She raised a brow. "Were you? I'm surprised."

He steadied his voice. "Just because I've opened four of these, doesn't make it any easier or less stressful. In fact, there is more pressure. From my brother to my business partners to my family, everyone has their reasons for wanting me to succeed."

"Do those reasons include stealing Lucy's jerk chicken recipe?" Jasmine accused. "That spice recipe is a family secret and one of the reasons why we've been so successful in the past."

"I didn't steal it," Micah said. "She gave it to me."

"I don't understand why. It's almost like she didn't trust me with it."

"That's not true," Micah insisted.

"Why else would she give it to you then? You both went behind my back."

Her voice softened with hurt, rather than jealousy, and he understood why she might feel that way.

"Please don't be upset with your grandmother. She came to me because she could see how stressed out you were about cooking. She wanted someone else besides Gloria to know the secret recipe, so she told me. Can you blame her?"

It took a few moments, but then Jasmine shook her head in resignation.

"I've gotten the hang of most of Lucy's recipes, with the exception of the jerk chicken. I guess I don't have the patience for cooking. I like the sales and marketing side of the restaurant business."

"Then stick with what you know, and let me help you with the rest."

She gave him a dubious look. "What do you mean?"

"I told Lucy I wanted to help you with the restaurant as much as possible, but I was afraid you would never forgive me for lying to you."

Jasmine smiled, and he felt his heart skip a beat.

"I do forgive you. I talked everything over with Lucy and I realize now that you didn't mean to hurt me. In some ways, your hands were tied."

Although he wanted to smother her with kisses, he gave her a grateful nod.

"I told you as soon as I could. I just wish I'd had the courage to confide in you sooner, but I was afraid of losing you. I know how important your grandmother's restaurant is to you."

"It is, but don't think I'm too altruistic and I'm certainly no saint. At first, moving to Bay Point was an excuse to run away from a painful experience. Over time, living and working with Lucy helped me to rediscover the meaning in my life. And then I met you—"

"And everything changed," Micah finished. "Despite my stupid mistakes and dishonesty, I hope it was for the better."

She nodded. "My life sharpened into focus. I'm more excited about the possibilities, and about my future."

"You mean it wasn't the great sex?" he joked.

Jasmine laughed, and the joyful sound made his throat catch.

"I'm sure that had something to do with it."

"I'm so sorry about everything, baby."

He took her into his arms and they kissed, long and hard, and a swell of emotion overtook them both.

"I've missed you so much. I don't ever want to be without you again."

"Nor do I, Micah. Promise me you won't leave me?"

"Not a chance. You're stuck with me."

She snuggled up against his chest and he nuzzled the top of her head.

"In fact, I've talked it over with the guys and they agreed. We want you to be our global head of marketing."

Jasmine gasped and stepped back. "Wait. What are you saying? Are you offering me a job?"

"Yes. You would not only be responsible for getting the word out about Society Red, but my partner's restaurants, too. We even plan to open a location in France next year."

Her eyes looked conflicted. "Micah, I don't know what to say."

He put his hands on her shoulders. "Just say yes. It's a great opportunity. You and I can stay in Bay Point and you can travel with me, whenever you want."

Jasmine turned away, walked to the window and stared across the street. "I know I should jump at the chance, but what about the restaurant?"

He joined her there and slid his arms around her waist. "We can redo the whole thing—inside and out, and serve breakfast, lunch and an assortment of your mouthwatering desserts, so there's no competition with Society Red. We can be partners, for life!"

Jasmine's chin shot up and there was a rush of unmistakable excitement in her voice, as she turned to face him.

"We? What's this 'we' business?"

"You'll still own the restaurant, of course," Micah continued, ignoring her inquiry as he gazed into her eyes. If he stopped talking, he feared he wouldn't get out the most important question of all.

"But we'll run it together when we're married. I'll help you be successful."

He paused for her answer. Her eyes were shiny and her lips were parted.

"You do want to marry me, don't you, Jasmine?"

Afraid that she was about to say no, he broke into her stunned silence and kissed her again. She leaned into him, murmuring his name against his lips.

Micah pulled away suddenly. "Wait, I almost forgot something."

He drew a ring from his pocket and took a deep breath, as his heart hammered away in his chest.

"I love you, Jasmine. I bought this for you while we were in New York on the chance that one day, you'd say yes."

Her eyes widened and she gasped at the size of the diamond as he held it up to her. Micah figured that if it was possible for Jasmine to feel happy, scared and amused, all at the same time, this moment was it.

"You knew you wanted this? Commitment? Even then?"

"And even more so now. I want to marry you, Jasmine."

He slipped the ring onto her finger, and was relieved when it was a perfect fit.

"You are my future, the only woman I want. I would be honored if you would be my wife."

She admired the ring, and then wrapped her arms around his neck, and hugged him tightly.

"Yes. I want to be your wife, Micah," she whispered. "I want to be your everything."

"You already are," Micah said, as he traced her lips with his fingers. "Thank you for forgiving me. I'm sure this won't be the last time."

"I love you."

The intensity of her words made him harden instantly.

"I love you so much, Jasmine. I can't wait to spend my whole life loving you."

"Then kiss me, Micah," she begged, closing her eyes, moist with tears.

Her body curved and moved against his, in a slow dance and a dream fulfilled, just for two.

"Kiss me, and don't stop!"

At the tender urgency in her voice, Micah lowered his mouth to hers, at first tentatively, then hungrily, greedily. His heart, so full of longing for this woman, and now, she was finally his.

* * * * *

COMING NEXT MONTH
Available May 22, 2018

#573 WHEN I'M WITH YOU

***The Lawsons of Louisiana* • by Donna Hill**

Longtime New Orleans bachelor Rafe Lawson is ready to tie the knot. His heart has been captured by the gorgeous Avery Richards. Then the media descends, jeopardizing her Secret Service career—and their imminent wedding. But it's the unexpected return of Rafe's first love that could cost the tycoon everything.

#574 PLEASURE IN HIS KISS

***Love in the Hamptons* • by Pamela Yaye**

Beauty blogger and owner of the Hamptons's hottest salon Karma Sullivan has been swept off her feet by judge Morrison Drake. But she knows their passion-filled nights must end. She can't let her family secret derail Morrison's ambitious career plan. Even if it means giving up the man she loves…

#575 TEMPTING THE BEAUTY QUEEN

***Once Upon a Tiara* • by Carolyn Hector**

If Kenzie Swayne didn't require a date for a string of upcoming weddings, she'd turn Ramon Torres's offer down flat. The gorgeous entrepreneur stood her up once already. Now Ramon needs Kenzie's expertise for a new business venture. But when past secrets are revealed, can Ramon make Kenzie his—forever?

#576 WHEREVER YOU ARE

***The Jacksons of Ann Arbor* • by Elle Wright**

Avery Montgomery created a hit show about her old neighborhood, but she can't reveal the real reason she left town. Dr. Elwood Jackson has never forgiven Avery for leaving. But when a crisis lands her in El's emergency room, passion sparks hotter than before. Will this be their second chance?

KPCNM0518

They were a natural fit with each other, as if living under the same roof was something they'd always done. Rafe was attentive, but gave her space. He possessed chef-like skills in the kitchen, a penchant for neatness—she never had to step over discarded clothing or clean up after a meal—and above all he was a master in the bedroom and made her see heaven on a regular basis. This man was going to be her husband. Sometimes, when she looked at him or held him tight between her thighs, she couldn't believe that Rafe Lawson was hers. What she wanted was just the two of them, but marrying Rafe was marrying his large, controlling family.

KPEXP0518

"You sure you'll be okay until I get back from N'awlins?" He wiped off the countertop with a damp cloth.

She shimmied onto the bar stool at the island counter and extended her hands to Rafe. He took two long steps and was in front of her. He raised her hands to his lips and kissed the insides of her palms.

"I'll be fine, and right here when you get back." She leaned in to kiss him.

"Hmm, I can change my plans," he said against her lips, "and stay here, which is what I'd rather do." He caressed her hips.

Avery giggled. "Me, too, but you've been gone long enough. Take care of your business."

He stepped deep between her legs. "Business can wait." He threaded his fingers through the hair at the nape of her neck, dipped his head and kissed her collarbone.

Avery sucked in a breath of desire and instinctively tightened her legs around him. "You're going to be late," she whispered.

He brushed his lips along her neck, nibbled the lobe of her ear. "Privilege is the perk of owning your own plane. Can't leave without me."

KPEXP0518

SPECIAL EXCERPT FROM

HARLEQUIN®

ROMANTIC suspense

Armstrong Black doesn't do partners, and Danielle Winstead is not a team player. To find the criminal they're after, they have to trust each other. But their powerful attraction throws an unexpected curveball in their investigation!

Read on for a sneak preview of
SEDUCED BY THE BADGE,
the first book in Deborah Fletcher Mello*'s*
new miniseries,
TO SEDUCE AND SERVE.

"Why did you leave your service revolver on my bathroom counter?" Armstrong asked as they stood at the bus stop, waiting for her return ride.

"I can't risk keeping it strapped on me and I was afraid one of the girls might go through my bag and find it. I knew it was safe with you."

"I don't like you not having your gun."

"I'll be fine. I have a black belt in karate and jujitsu. I know how to take care of myself!"

Armstrong nodded. "So you keep telling me. It doesn't mean I'm not going to worry about you, though."

Danni rocked back and forth on her heels. Deep down she was grateful that a man did care. For longer than she wanted to admit, there hadn't been a man who did.

Armstrong interrupted her thoughts. "There's a protective detail already in front of the coffee shop and another that will follow you and your bus. There will be someone on you at all times. If you get into any trouble, you know what to do."

Danni nodded. "I'll contact you as soon as it's feasible. And please, if there is any change in Alissa's condition, find a way to let me know."

"I will. I promise."

Danni's attention shifted to the bus that had turned the corner and was making its way toward them. A wave of sadness suddenly rippled through her stomach.

"You good?" Armstrong asked, sensing the change in her mood.

She nodded, biting back the rise of emotion. "I'll be fine," she answered.

As the bus pulled up to the stop, he drew her hand into his and pulled it to his mouth, kissing the backs of her fingers.

Danni gave him one last smile as she fell into line with the others boarding the bus. She tossed a look over her shoulder as he stood staring after her. The woman in front of her was pushing an infant in a stroller. A boy about eight years old and a little girl about five clung to each side of the carriage. The little girl looked back at Danni and smiled before hiding her face in her mother's skirt. The line stopped, an elderly woman closer to the front struggling with a multitude of bags to get inside.

She suddenly spun around, the man behind her eyeing her warily. "Excuse me," she said as she pushed past him and stepped aside. She called after Armstrong as she hurried back to where he stood.

"What's wrong?" he said as she came to a stop in front of him

"Nothing," Danni said as she pressed both palms against his broad chest. "Nothing at all." She lifted herself up on her toes as her gaze locked with his. Her hands slid up his chest to the sides of his face. She gently cupped her palms against his cheeks and then she pressed her lips to his.

Don't miss
SEDUCED BY THE BADGE by Deborah Fletcher Mello,
available June 2018 wherever
Harlequin® Romantic Suspense books and ebooks are sold.

HRSEXP0518